slipped in without anyone noticing me. His office was next to his secretary's, but as there was only a light showing under his door, I knew he was alone.

'As I went in, he looked very startled — perhaps because Diana and I are rather alike. However, he saw it wasn't my sister of course, and soon began to put on his old act. He pretended that seeing me was a nice surprise. Then I moved a pace or two into the room and he saw the revolver I took from my handbag. He knew about Diana's death, and realized why I had come.'

She paused, re-enacting the scene in her mind.

'I pressed the trigger . . . his expression changed . . . he crumpled up and his head fell on the desk as if he were terribly tired. My mind appeared to go blank for a minute — I might have screamed for all I know — then I came to my senses — and listened. I expected to see someone come running in, but nobody did. Suddenly, I realized that the band in the dance room at the end of the corridor was playing very loudly — they must have drowned the noise of the shot.

'Somehow, that raucous dance music seemed to make it all the more horrible. I panicked. All I wanted to do was to get away from — him — ' She paused, moistening her lips, and nervously snapping the clasp of her bag. 'I opened the door and looked down the corridor. It was deserted, and I had no trouble in finding my way out. I don't know how I got back to my flat . . . and I've been expecting the police ever since. I meant to give myself up this morning — and then, in the paper I read this — '

Out of her bag she took a newspaper cutting and handed it to him. It was an account of Max Power's death, and the headline ran: 'NIGHT CLUB OWNER FOUND SHOT — LEAVES SUICIDE NOTE . . . '

He regarded her pensively. 'And has this newspaper report had any effect on your plans?'

'Well yes,' she admitted. 'It's made me undecided. I didn't know what to do. I killed Max — but according to that report he was going to kill himself anyway.'

'You mean,' Doctor Morelle asked, 'that you merely performed a task he was about to perform for himself?

She looked at him imploringly. 'Don't you see? Do I have to pay the penalty for killing a man who intended to commit suicide? A man who deserved to die in any case? The man who drove my sister to her death. Surely if I can escape the penalty for what I've done, I'm entitled to. Haven't I suffered enough as it is?'

Doctor Morelle reflected, then said: 'Well as for that, I can't advise you. I'm a psychiatrist not a lawyer. Nor am I a judge.'

'Please help me,' the girl begged. 'What can I do?'

'Have you come to me because you think I will set your conscience at rest? Because you want me to tell you that it's perfectly all right for you to keep silent?' Doctor Morelle paused, then went on harshly: 'You have confessed that you have taken another human being's life. You admit that you've killed a man whom you once loved and you believe loved you — '

'Doctor Morelle, please — !'

'You murdered him and now, because of some fortuitous chance which has completely transformed the situation, you ask me to soothe your troubled mind, smooth away your fears so that you can go on living as if nothing has ever happened. Supposing I said that you must go to the police and tell them what you've told me. What then, Miss Webb?

'I don't know,' the girl said miserably, her head bowed. 'You don't understand. He drove me to it.'

'I do understand your point of view,' the Doctor said, and she looked up at him in surprise, hope dawning on her drawn face.

'After you shot him, he fell forward onto his desk. Did you move the body?

The girl looked surprised. 'No, I couldn't even have touched it.'

'What about his suicide note? You saw no trace of it when you went into his room?'

'I didn't notice any particular paper. There was a mass of them on his desk. I was only thinking of getting my revenge.'

'Do you think Powers was the sort of man who would commit suicide?' he suddenly demanded.

She bit hit lip. 'I don't know. I shouldn't have thought so.'

'Were you ever aware that he was in financial difficulties?'

'He never discussed money with me — but he never seemed to be short.'

His keen gaze seemed to penetrate her brain.

'Do you really think he'd have gone through with this suicide if you hadn't shot him?'

'Well, he had written a note.'

'Hundreds of people do that, and lack the courage for the final act.' For some seconds, neither spoke. Then he asked:

'As a matter of interest, Miss Webb, how did the gun come into your possession?

'I . . . I borrowed it from a man in the fashion business. His hobby was collecting guns. I met him through Max. At first he was reluctant to lend me a gun — he told me that I should consult you instead, and gave me a card with your phone number and address. But when I insisted, he eventually agreed.'

'I see,' Doctor Morelle nodded. 'What's his name and address?

'His name is Baker . . . Ellis Baker. His address is 16 Sloane Place, off Sloane Street.

Doctor Morelle jotted down the details on his pad.

'But why,' the girl asked unhappily, 'are you asking me all this if you're not going to help me?'

'On the contrary, Miss Webb, it occurs to me that this matter requires probing a little more deeply. There are several puzzling anomalies in this case that need to be resolved. No doubt certain salient facts will emerge at the inquest, which is to be held tomorrow. I think you may well postpone your confession for a while.'

Paula Webb looked alarmed. 'You don't mean that I will have to attend that inquest and — '

'No, I don't mean that at all. I suggest you simply remain at home until I contact you again. In that regard, please leave your address and phone number with

Miss Frayle before you go. You will do that?'

She nodded dumbly.

He scribbled on a form on his desk. 'A prolonged sleep would be of great benefit to you. If you will get this prescription made up by your chemist . . . ' He handed her the paper, which she accepted gratefully.

'You mean . . . Dr. Morelle, I don't have to go to the police?'

'I mean, Miss Webb, that this seems to be a case for me after all!'

★   ★   ★

The following day, the Coroner was doing his summing up at the official inquest into the death of Max Powers.

'As I said when this inquest opened, members of the jury, you are here to enquire into the circumstances surrounding the death of Mr. Max Powers.

'All the relevant witnesses have been called. You have heard all the evidence. And now it is your duty to give your verdict as representatives of the public.

'You've listened carefully I'm sure. And it is quite plain how this unfortunate man met his death. Was he so tormented by some secret fear or anxiety, which rendered him emotionally unstable at the time that he decided to take his own life? That is what you have to decide. Now will you please retire and consider your verdict.'

There came a shuffling of feet as the jury retired.

Inspector Hood turned to Doctor Morelle. 'What do you think of it, Doctor?'

'I imagine they won't be long reaching their verdict,' Doctor Morelle said thoughtfully.

Inspector Hood nodded. 'Pretty clear cut really.'

'I thought you presented the facts as you saw them plainly enough.'

'Thanks, Doctor.' The Inspector glanced across to where the dead man's black-clad widow was seated. 'Poor Mrs. Powers has stood up to the ordeal well,' he commented.

Doctor Morelle followed his gaze, and

frowned slightly. 'You mentioned that she'd been his secretary before she married Powers?'

'Yes, that was about seven years ago, I believe,' Hood affirmed.

'I wonder if I might glance at the letter he wrote to her?'

'Yes, here it is.' The Inspector handed it over. 'He left it in the machine after he'd typed it.'

Doctor Morelle read aloud: ''I can't go on any longer. Life has become too much for me. I just can't take it any more. There's nothing left but this way out.

''Goodbye, darling. Max'.'

'I can only assume that some secret worry or something got him down,' Hood said.

'So it would appear . . . ' The Doctor held out the note, and pointed to a word. 'Odd spelling that, did you notice?'

'Where?' Hood craned forward. 'Oh, that word. He must have forgotten to add the 'e'. People do that sometimes — ' he broke off as there came the sounds of the jury returning. He smiled faintly. 'Yes, you were right, Doctor Morelle. The jury haven't taken long.'

'Mrs. Powers has gone very pale,' Doctor Morelle commented, looking across at her.

The Coroner cleared his throat, then asked: 'Members of the jury, have you considered your verdict?'

'Yes, sir,' the Jury Foreman responded. 'We find that Max Powers killed himself while the balance of his mind was disturbed.'

As the verdict was delivered, Mrs. Powers gave an audible groan, and slumped in her chair.

Doctor Morelle, who had been watching her closely, was instantly on his feet and moved across to her. 'Let me help you,' he murmured.

'She's fainted, Doctor!' Hood exclaimed, coming alongside.

'Yes, she has,' Doctor Morelle agreed thoughtfully, supporting her under her arms as she sat slumped in her seat.

'It's been pretty grim for her, poor thing,' Hood muttered sympathetically.

Doctor Morelle turned to one of the officials who were beginning to come forward. 'Open that window, will you? Get some air to her . . .'

★ ★ ★

At Doctor Morelle's Harley Street address Miss Frayle was answering the telephone.

'Hello. This is Doctor Morelle's house. No, he's not. Yes, he's gone to the inquest. All right — ' She broke off as the door opened.

'Doctor Morelle! You're back,' she exclaimed.

'Observant of you,' he murmured dryly.

Miss Frayle replaced the telephone with a long sigh. 'Those newspaper reporters have never stopped phoning. Was the verdict suicide?'

Doctor Morelle nodded. 'That was a foregone conclusion, the coroner not being in possession of certain facts known to us.'

'I've had an idea,' Miss Frayle began.

'Some coffee, Miss Frayle, don't you think?'

'I'll get some, but first I must tell you . . .'

Doctor Morelle sighed heavily. 'Miss Frayle, no doubt your theory is most absorbing . . . '

Miss Frayle tightened her lips. 'Oh well, of course, if you'd rather not know the answer, I don't want to force it on you. I mean you just plod on in your own way.'

Doctor Morelle refused to take the bait. Instead he took her at her word. 'Thank you. I want to make a few notes and then perhaps I could have some coffee.'

Miss Frayle accepted defeat. 'All right, I'm ready to take notes.'

'At the inquest this morning Inspector Hood reaffirmed what he mentioned to us in Park Lane the night before last, making crystal clear what I'd already surmised, which was that Max Powers was found not in his own office, but in his secretary's adjoining. And on the face of it, that he'd taken his own life . . . '

Miss Frayle frowned. 'Yes, but . . . '

'I am gratified that you agree with me,' Doctor Morelle cut her short. 'But against this apparently indisputable evidence, we have Miss Webb's revelation.'

Miss Frayle was determined to make

her observations. 'But it's so perfectly simple,' she said. 'She made the whole thing up. She's madly infatuated with him. She got this guilt complex because of the wife, and then her sister — '

'This is fascinating,' Doctor Morelle said heavily. 'But you appear to have overlooked the fact that Miss Webb's action was premeditated. She borrowed a gun for the purpose.'

Miss Frayle frowned. 'Oh, I hadn't thought of that.'

'Every word of her account rings true and that is where its significance lies. She described how she shot Powers in his office. He fell across his own desk, where she left him — and yet he was discovered at the desk in his *secretary's* office next door . . . '

'But Doctor Morelle, who moved the body?'

'And why?' he added.

Miss Frayle puzzled for several moments, then said brightly:

'I've just thought of something. She *did* fire at him as she said, but she missed.'

'I had considered that possibility and

rejected it,' Doctor Morelle was emphatic. 'There would have been visible damage caused by the bullet. The police examined both rooms but found only one bullet in the deceased.'

Miss Frayle waved her hands. 'Oh, I just don't understand it.'

'Which reminds me, since I'm not going to get that coffee . . . '

'Oh, Doctor . . . ' Miss Frayle looked contrite.

'It's too late now, there's something more pressing.' Doctor Morelle got to his feet. 'Yes, I think perhaps you'd better accompany me.'

Miss Frayle goggled. 'Where are we going?'

'To 16 Sloane Place.'

'That's where Ellis Baker lives,' Miss Frayle said wonderingly. 'The man who lent her the gun.'

'Precisely, my dear Miss Frayle.'

★ ★ ★

Ellis Baker was at home, and invited his visitors to enter.

'How remiss of me not to recognise you at once, Doctor Morelle,' he was saying as he showed them to his living room. 'I've heard and read a lot about you.'

Doctor Morelle smiled thinly. 'This is Miss Frayle, my secretary.'

'How do you do?' she said.

'Delighted to meet you Miss Frayle,' Baker said, shaking hands politely.

Doctor Morelle had already pushed into the room, his attention captured by a framed picture on the mantelpiece. 'What a charming photograph you have there,' he said, pointing to it.

'Why, it's *her*.' Miss Frayle blinked.

'Paula Webb — you know her?' Baker asked.

'We have met,' Doctor Morelle said dryly.

Baker frowned slightly. 'Is it on account of her that you're here?'

Doctor Morelle smiled faintly. 'You're quite the mind reader, Mr. Baker.'

'What is this about Paula?' There was a slightly defensive tone in Baker's voice.

'I understand you lent her a revolver,' Doctor Morelle said levelly.

'So that's it.' Baker looked at him. 'You're not telling me she's made a fool of herself with it?'

Doctor Morelle didn't answer directly. Instead he asked: 'Didn't you think it was risky to lend Miss Webb a loaded revolver?'

Baker gave a curious smile and relaxed somewhat. He turned to one of a number of display cases on a long side table. 'Do you think so? She asked me, so I lent her one. A Smith and Wesson Centennial, it fires a .38 calibre cartridge. If that's what you've come to ask. There is one just like it.' Reaching into the case, he extracted the weapon and broke open the chamber, displaying the contents to the Doctor. 'And these are the cartridges.'

'These are what you gave her to use?' Doctor Morelle questioned sharply.

'That's right.'

'I see. Most illuminating.' Looking at Doctor Morelle curiously, Miss Frayle thought she had detected a gleam in his eye as he spoke.

'I let her have three rounds,' Baker said, 'She admitted she didn't know a great deal about handling a revolver, but I imagined it would give her confidence.'

Doctor Morelle nodded. 'Most thoughtful of you. You were acquainted with Max Powers, were you not?'

'So Paula has been talking to you,' Baker shrugged. 'Yes, I knew him and his wife. Why?'

'As you say, Miss Webb has been talking.'

Baker frowned. 'Is she trying to say it wasn't suicide . . . that someone bumped him off?'

'What makes you think that idea might have occurred to her?' Doctor Morelle asked sharply.

Baker tightened his lips, and lost his easy-going geniality. 'Listen, Doctor Morelle, you didn't call here just to chat about Paula Webb or my collection of pistols. Max Powers was a first-rate heel. If someone's murdered him and got away with it, good luck to them. I wish I could have done it. Anything else I can tell you before you go?'

Doctor Morelle shook his head. 'No, You've been most informative.'

Baker relaxed somewhat. 'Only too glad. Goodbye, Miss Frayle.

'Goodbye, Mr. Baker.'

'And goodbye, to you, Doctor Morelle — or should we say *au revoir*?'

Doctor Morelle smiled thinly. 'That rather depends upon events.'

Baker laughed. 'So we'll just make it so long, eh?'

After they had left his flat, Miss Frayle looked at Doctor Morelle accusingly. 'You didn't breathe a word to him, Doctor Morelle! How she could think she'd shot him and all the time she hadn't.'

'It was that somewhat mystifying feature which prompted the visit to Baker,' he murmured suavely.

Miss Frayle was still unsatisfied. 'Who told you nothing except that he had lent her the gun. And that he took a dim view of Max Powers.'

'It was not so much what he said, but what I *saw*,' the Doctor informed her enigmatically.

'Oh, I didn't see anything. It was a beautiful flat . . . and well, there was her photo . . . and, oh, all those guns.'

'He confirmed it was the firearm that she described.'

'Which you never told him she'd lost . . . ' Miss Frayle shrugged. 'Anyway, he's got plenty more.'

'What interested me were the cartridges, which he'd given her.'

'Well, I didn't bother to look at them,' Miss Frayle admitted frankly.

Doctor Morelle smiled sardonically. 'Had you done so, even *you* might have noticed one stimulating fact about them.'

Miss Frayle bristled a little at the biting sarcasm, but her curiosity got the better of her finer feelings. 'All right, Dr. Morelle, what was it?

'*They were blanks*, Miss Frayle!'

★　★　★

Miss Frayle answered the ringing of the doorbell at Doctor Morelle's house in Harley Street. She gave a little start of surprise when she opened the door.

'Oh, Miss Webb . . . '

'I've got to see him!' Tight-lipped,

Paula Webb pushed past Miss Frayle into the hallway.

Miss Frayle fluttered helplessly. 'But, oh, Miss Webb . . . come back. Oh, Doctor Morelle *will* be annoyed . . . ' She closed the door carefully.

Meantime, knowing the way from her previous visit, Paula Webb was already confronting Doctor Morelle.

' . . . it was here in the early evening papers,' she was saying. 'in the stop press. Look: '4.00 p.m. news. New turn in Park Lane death. Understood Scotland Yard not satisfied with results of earlier enquiries into death of Max Powers of Mayfair Nightclub found shot in his office three nights ago. As a result of information received, renewed investigations being made into circumstances of the tragedy'.' She looked at him accusingly. 'The police have found out that he was murdered after all!'

Doctor Morelle regarded her calmly. 'Well, I'm glad you called, Miss Webb,' he said suavely. 'There are one or two matters I think you might care to know about.'

'What have you done?' the girl demanded.

The Doctor smiled faintly. 'If your anxiety is on account of that newspaper report, then you may relax.'

Paula Webb frowned in perplexity. 'But the only person who could have made them change their mind is you! I came to see you for help and all you've done — '

He raised a deprecating hand. 'Let me assure you that your own situation is in no way jeopardized, and — '

He broke off as the door opened.

Miss Frayle entered the room timorously. 'Oh, Doctor Morelle, I'm so sorry.'

He ignored her apology. Instead, he said crisply: 'Miss Frayle, what was it I was to explain to Miss Webb?'

'Oh, you mean about . . . about . . . ' Miss Frayle's voiced trailed off uncertainly.

'You couldn't be more explicit?' Doctor Morelle sighed as Miss Frayle still hesitated. He turned to Paula Webb. 'What Miss Frayle means is that it was impossible for you to have killed Max Powers.'

'But I shot him!'

Miss Frayle finally found her voice. 'No . . . no, Doctor Morelle's right. Mr. Baker only gave you blank cartridges.'

A look of amazement crossed the girl's face. 'Blank cartridges?'

'He thought you might get into trouble,' Miss Frayle explained, 'so when you fired them they were only blanks.'

'But he . . . ' Paula Webb was struggling to accept what she had been told. 'I saw him fall!'

Doctor Morelle smiled thinly. 'He merely fainted from shock: he had a weak heart. After he had recovered consciousness, someone else took a hand.'

'You mean someone else killed him?' the girl asked incredulously.

Doctor Morelle nodded. 'That is the most logical explanation. Now, Miss Frayle, take Miss Webb into the other room. I have some important phone calls to make.'

Miss Frayle stepped forward and took the girl's elbow. 'Yes, Doctor Morelle.'

'I still can't believe . . . '

'Come along,' Miss Frayle gently directed her towards the door. 'I'll make you a cup of tea.'

'Oh, Miss Frayle . . . '

Doctor Morelle's secretary looked back into the room as she was about to close the door. 'Yes, Doctor?'

'Please ask Miss Webb to lend you her key to the *Night Owl* Club, before she leaves.'

'Her key?'

'Yes. And one more thing: you may care to accompany me on a visit I shall be paying tonight.'

'Oh, yes,' Miss Frayle said wonderingly. She closed the door and turned to the dazed Paula Webb. 'Come along, Miss Webb. You've been under a great cloud, but it's all over.'

In his study, Docrtor Morelle reached for the telephone on his desk.

'Now,' he murmured, 'first, Inspector Hood, then . . . '

★ ★ ★

Outside Doctor Morelle's Harley Steet address, a taxi driver glanced back over his shoulder.

43

'Where to?'

From the back seat of the cab, Miss Frayle answered promptly. 'Archway House, Park Lane, please.'

Beside her, Doctor Morelle murmured, 'Thank you, Miss Frayle.'

'You don't think anything could go wrong, Doctor?' she asked anxiously.

'I fail to see why,' he answered calmly. 'The trap has been carefully baited.'

'And they'll walk right into it?'

'It's a matter of process of elimination. The motive fits and the opportunity.' Doctor Morelle spoke with complete certainty. 'Above all else, who would have thought of typing that farewell letter?'

Miss Frayle settled in her seat. 'Anyway, we shall know for certain in a little while.'

After a short journey, Doctor Morelle leaned forward.

'This corner please driver.'

The taxi stopped and they got out. Doctor Morelle paid the driver. 'Thank you, sir,' he responded warmly to his tip, and drove off

Miss Frayle looked about her in the

dark street, then up at the short flight of steps leading to the back entrance of the *Night Owl* Club. 'You've got the key Miss Webb gave us? Oh, it's very dark . . . '

'Would you prefer it if I left you here?' Doctor Morelle asked.

'Oh, no, no. I'll come with you.'

'I'm flattered by your trust in me,' he said dryly.

They entered the building. It was completely deserted, Mrs. Powers having closed the night club — for the time being, at least — as a mark of respect to her late husband.

There was just enough light casting along the corridor through the frosted glass panel in the top of the door to enable them to see their way, following the directions Paula Webb had given them.

'The office would be this way,' Miss Frayle whispered. 'Oh, it's awfully eerie. This is the door . . . next to his office.'

They entered the office of the late Max Powers' secretary.

'I suppose we can't switch on the light?' Miss Frayle asked.

'You suppose right,' Doctor Morelle said briefly.

'What do we do now?'

'We wait.'

'Oh, I didn't know it was going to be quite like this,' Miss Frayle said nervously.

'Quiet . . . listen!' Doctor Morelle commanded.

Approaching footsteps sounded along the corridor. The door opened slowly, and a hand sought — and found — the light switch.

Miss Frayle gave an audible sigh as she recognized a familiar figure..

'Oh . . . Oh, it's you Inspector Hood.'

'Hello. So you got here before me.'

'You know exactly how events will proceed?' Doctor Morelle asked him.

Hood nodded imperceptibly. 'Yes, thanks to you.'

'Better put out that light again.'

'Right,' Hood murmured, and the office was again plunged into darkness.

'You never mentioned him coming, Doctor Morelle,' Miss Frayle whispered accusingly.

'The Inspector is part of the trap.'

They waited in silence for several minutes, then there came the sound of more footsteps approaching the office.

A female voice sounded from outside the door, which was slowly pushed open. 'Is anyone there?'

'All right, Hood,' Doctor Morelle said crisply.

The Inspector switched on the light as the woman came into the office. 'Good evening, Mrs. Powers,' he said levelly.

Mrs. Powers looked about her confusedly. 'What is this? I . . . why, you're Doctor Morelle!'

He gave a slight nod of his head. 'I regret having to disappoint you.'

She stared at him accusingly. 'So it was *you* who phoned me. You who pretended you thought you could blackmail me!'

Doctor Morelle smiled sardonically. 'I had to get you here by hook or by crook.'

Mrs. Powers glared at him. 'What have you got me here for?

Inspector Hood pointed to a typewriter on the secretary's desk. 'Just you type a little letter, Mrs. Powers.'

She stared at him blankly. 'What are you talking about?'

Moving to one side of the desk, Inspector Hood said, 'You can type, can't you?'

'Even with your gloves on in order not to leave any fingerprints,' Doctor Morelle challenged.

'I don't know what you're getting at,' Mrs. Powers faltered.

Doctor Morelle placed his hand on the woman's elbow and guided her across to the desk. Dazedly, she allowed herself to be settled into the chair. 'I'll tell you what to put. Just a very brief letter. Miss Frayle, put some paper in the machine.'

'Yes, Doctor.' Miss Frayle inserted a sheet of paper into the typewriter and expertly adjusted the roller, before standing to one side.

'It's up to you, Mrs. Powers,' Inspector Hood said. 'If you're innocent, you've got nothing to fear.'

Mrs. Powers began to recover her poise. 'Of course I'm innocent!' she snapped. 'Max killed himself.'

'Then take a letter,' Hood said.

'Very well.' Mrs. Powers spoke defiantly.

Doctor Morelle began to dictate: 'I can't go on any longer — stop — Life has become too much for me — stop — I just can't take it any more — stop — There is nothing left but this way out — stop — Goodbye darling — stop — Max.'

Mrs. Powers looked up frowningly as she finished typing the letter. 'This is what *he* wrote.'

Doctor Morelle leaned forward and extracted the letter from the machine: He glanced at it, then smiled thinly. 'Is it? Isn't it what *you* wrote?' He held out the letter so that the Inspector could read it. 'Hood, there it is again.'

Hood read from the last part of the typed letter: 'Goodbye darling, and you've typed it the same way. G-O-O-D-B-Y *but without the* 'e".'

'What do you mean?' Mrs. Powers protested. 'I've always . . . '

'Exactly, Mrs. Powers,' Doctor Morelle said harshly. 'You've always spelt goodbye without the final 'e'.'

Mrs. Powers collapsed over the desk, sobbing.

Thereafter, under skilful questioning from Doctor Morelle, she made a full confession of guilt, with Miss Frayle enterprisingly making shorthand notes. The picture that emerged confirmed Doctor Morelle's deductions.

After her husband had recovered from his first collapse — when he'd fainted because he thought he'd been shot — he had telephoned his wife, asking her to bring round some of his heart tablets. On arrival, she had seen the gun — which Max had picked up from the floor and left on his desk — and demanded to know exactly what had happened. He had prevaricated at first, but when she had threatened to withhold the tablets he needed for his weak heart, he told her about Paula's visit, and what she had told him.

He'd been playing her up for years with other women and she'd forgiven him. But when she heard that Paula's sister had committed suicide through him, she snapped. In her jealous rage she had evolved her plan. She got him to go into the secretarial office next door on the pretext of finding a glass of water for his tablets, then she shot him with her own automatic. She had worn gloves. Positioning his body across his secretary's desk, she had typed the fake suicide note, and dropped her automatic on the floor nearby. Paula's weapon she had removed from the adjoining office and taken back with her.

★   ★   ★

It was an hour later. Inspector Hood had charged Mrs. Powers and taken her into custody. Doctor Morelle and Miss Frayle had declined his offer of transport and elected to walk back to Harley Street.

'I like walking along Park Lane at night,' Miss Frayle murmured, 'don't you Doctor?'

'The fresh air is certainly welcome.'

'Mmm, after all that went on in that office you mean. It's incredible to think that Max Powers encompassed his own doom when he telephoned his wife.'

51

Doctor Morelle smiled coldly. 'There was a certain irony to the events.'

'And you don't think Mr. Baker knew?' Miss Frayle asked.

Doctor Morelle shrugged. 'I believe he suspected, but he obviously felt that her husband deserved what he got.'

'Anyway, it's for Inspector Hood to sort out. You've done your part.'

'Thank you, Miss Frayle.'

'All because she discovered about Paula Webb and her sister,' Miss Frayle said. 'But I must say I still don't know how you were so sure it was Mrs. Powers!'

'I wasn't, at first,' Dr. Morelle admitted. 'Although a number of facts began to emerge which pointed to her — the jealous wife obviously, her reaction to the verdict at the inquest. Did she faint in the knowledge that she was unsuspected? And then I telephoned her masquerading as someone who had discovered the truth and that she would have to buy my silence. When she agreed to talk it over with me, I was sure.'

'Fancy her meeting you at the very place that she shot her husband,' Miss

Frayle said wonderingly.

Doctor Morelle stopped and gripped her arm. 'Don't you understand, my dear Miss Frayle?'

'Well, of course I do, Dr. Morelle. How do you mean?'

'She had to return to the scene of her crime,' he explained sententiously. 'Like any other criminal, she found herself subconsciously compelled to give herself away.'

'Oh, I see.' Miss Frayle frowned. 'I think.'

'She had to confess. Just as with any criminal, an inner compulsion forced Mrs. Powers to bring upon herself her own doom.'

# 2

## The Case of the Kidnapped Child

Doctor Morelle first attended Mrs. Carter as the result of an urgent and agitated telephone call one morning in the very early hours from her husband. Accompanied by Miss Frayle, he arrived at the Carters' house situated in an exclusive square off Park Lane. Miss Frayle rang the bell and after a few moments the door was opened by a butler of such repulsive aspect that she drew back with a gasp of apprehension.

'Wot yer ringing for?' the man demanded.

'Presumably with the object of attracting your attention,' murmured the Doctor, eyeing him with abstract interest. He was conjecturing what Lombroso might have made of the physiognomy before him.

'You Morelle?'

'I am Doctor Morelle.'

The butler glowered at him for a

moment then turned his menacing gaze upon Miss Frayle, who shrank back behind the Doctor. Then he growled reluctantly: 'Uh . . . Come in both you . . .'

Doctor Morelle, followed by Miss Frayle, who could not refrain from goggling at the man in morbid fascination, entered. The door closed behind them.

'Wait in here,' was the grunted instruction, and they found themselves in a luxuriously appointed library.

'I'll tell him,' the butler growled, and left them abruptly. As the door closed after him Miss Frayle exclaimed:

'What a horrible man!'

The Doctor lit a cigarette.

'A noteworthy subject for the anthropologist,' he mused. 'Quite remarkably Simian characteristics and abnormally long arms.'

'Like a gorilla, d'you mean?'

He bestowed upon her a supercilious smile: 'Precisely, Miss Frayle!'

At that moment the door opened and a plump, middle-aged man came in. His face appeared harassed. His voice, as he came towards them, was quiet with undertones of anxiety in it

'Doctor Morelle? I'm Carter.'

The Doctor nodded. 'This is my assistant, Miss Frayle,' he said. Carter gave her a wan smile.

'It's an unearthly hour,' he apologised, 'and I'm afraid you'll think it's the — well — ' he hesitated, and then went on quickly 'the police — I should really have sent for.'

'Police?' Miss Frayle blinked at him behind her spectacles.

The Doctor raised his eyebrows slightly. He surveyed the tip of his cigarette attentively. 'You intimated over the telephone,' he murmured, 'that your wife was in a state of collapse?'

'Yes ... You see — ' again the hesitation and words blurted out ' — our little girl has disappeared — she's been kidnapped!'

'Kidnapped?' breathed Miss Frayle.

'When did this occur?' Doctor Morelle queried.

'About an hour ago. My wife went to

the nursery to see if she was asleep, and she'd vanished.'

'Why *didn't* you send for the police?'

There was a perceptible pause. He considered the Doctor, as if weighing him up. Then he seemed to come to a decision. He squared his shoulders and said slowly: 'Doctor Morelle . . . I must explain . . . My wife is not a happy woman.' He passed his hand across his brow with a gesture of anxiety and doubt. With a muttered apology he beckoned them to sit down. The Doctor remained standing, however, and waited expectantly for Carter to continue. After a moment he began, leaning forward in his chair, and talking quickly and earnestly. His story was one that was not unfamiliar to the Doctor's ears.

Bella Carter was thirty-four when he had married her, and they had not considered the possibility of having children. When, however, a child, Sally, was born a change began to manifest itself in the Carter household, imperceptible at first and slow in development, but growing in intensity. She had suffered

57

considerable nervous strain during the birth of the child, and her convalescence was prolonged. During this time she actually saw very little of Sally, pleading that the baby's crying tried her nerves.

So the child's early years were spent chiefly in the company of nursemaids and that of her father. He had been delighted at her arrival, and began to spend more and more time with her as she reached an interesting age. Sally held an increasing fascination for him. On arriving back from the City, his first visit would be to the nursery. Nevertheless, and in spite of the breach that was growing palpably wider between them, he remained affectionate in his relationship with his wife.

Bella began to nurse a grievance. She had more time to brood now that her husband's business prospered and he became wealthier and correspondingly generous to her. She had all that she wanted in a material sense. Servants, clothes, her own car, an attractive town house and a lovely rambling old place in Sussex. And yet all the time she was weaving the pattern of her life into a highly tragic melodrama, with herself in the leading role of the wronged and neglected wife and mother.

Not unnaturally her attitude became responsible for her husband focusing his attention and affection increasingly upon his daughter. This in turn heightened Bella's persecution complex. More and more she imagined herself the innocent victim of almost every sort of malicious action. And so the vicious circle was tragically completed. It was not in her nature to suppress her highly-coloured imaginings. All her life Bella had drama-tised every passing fancy that flitted through her somewhat shallow mind. It had always given her considerable satisfaction. Moreover, such flights of histrionics had, in the early days of his marriage, never failed to achieve their object where her husband was concerned. Lately, as her dark imaginings became almost continuous, he was becoming somewhat inured to them and inclined to discount her extravagant assertions. Like a drug addict increasing the dose, she became more violent and outrageous; her actions became more eccentric in her frantic bid to steal the limelight from her daughter, now an attractive child.

'How old is your daughter?' the Doctor asked him as Carter came to the end of his story.

'Just five.'

'Poor little thing!' sympathised Miss Frayle.

'An only child,' continued Carter. 'I'm passionately devoted to her, but I was determined she should not be spoilt. That was the origin of the estrangement between my wife and me — '

He was about to go on, when Doctor Morelle suddenly raised his hand for silence, and moved swiftly across to the door. Noiselessly, he grasped the knob and turned it, flinging the door open with the same movement.

The huge figure of the butler jerked up from what was palpably a listening attitude. Miss Frayle was unable to suppress a tiny scream.

'I thought my intuition was not without foundation,' the Doctor murmured, eyeing the man with a sardonic smile.

'Riley! What d'you want?' demanded Carter sharply.

'I — er — I was — just — '

'Indulging in a little eavesdropping, possibly?' suggested Doctor Morelle, helpfully.

'I dunno what yer mean!'

Carter dismissed him with an impatient wave of his hand.

'I'll ring when I need you,' he said curtly. When the manservant had gone on his way muttering to himself, Carter turned to Doctor Morelle.

'I must apologise, Doctor. Riley's rather unconventional.'

'Quite!'

'I'd get rid of him, but Mrs. Carter won't hear of it.' He sighed heavily. 'This house seems to become more complicated every day!'

'Perhaps I might see your wife now?' queried the Doctor.

'Of course! Er — she'll be in her bedroom.' He paused. 'I know you are accustomed to somewhat strange cases, Doctor, but perhaps I ought to warn you — you may find my wife's room somewhat — er — unusual. Dark draperies . . . burning incense . . . and — er — well a coffin for a bed.'

'A coffin?' echoed Miss Frayle wonderingly.

'She insists on it — won't sleep anywhere else,' said the other with a shrug as if apologising for his wife's unaccountable behaviour.

The Doctor gave him a shrewd look, an interested expression in his narrow eyes.

'H'm . . . doubtless some inhibition connected with some obscure fixation complex.'

'If you'll follow me,' said Carter. He moved to the door with some reluctance. This time there was no eavesdropping figure in the doorway.

'Thank goodness that man's gone,' whispered Miss Frayle.

'Not for goodness I should imagine!' came back Doctor Morelle's swift retort.

'This way,' called Carter, turning and beckoning them up a fine oak staircase. 'My wife's room is on the other side of the house.'

He led the way along a wide corridor

with polished floors. Presently they came to a room that seemed to stand on its own in a corner of the house. For a second he paused outside the door, as if nerving himself to face an ordeal. Then he knocked gently and called:

'Bella! Bella! Doctor Morelle's here . . . '

There was no reply, but the Doctor thought he detected the sound of a swift movement inside the room.

'We'll go in,' said Carter softly. He opened the door.

If he had not forewarned them, the room might have indeed proved startling, with its heavy black and purple drapings, subdued light and unusual furniture. Everywhere the oppressive smell of incense.

But the Doctor's attention was rapidly directed to the fact that the huge manservant was standing at the foot of the coffin in which a woman was languidly reclining. His attitude could only be described as aggressive.

'Riley, send them away — I don't want to see any doctor!' complained the voice from the coffin.

'Yes, madam!' growled the butler, directing a dark look towards the Doctor and Miss Frayle.

'Now, now, my dear . . . ' began Carter persuasively, moving towards her.

'Go away, all of you!' cried Mrs. Carter, her voice high-pitched and melodramatic. 'Leave me in my grief!'

'Perhaps I might help,' suggested Doctor Morelle, stepping forward, and concentrating his gaze upon her. As he did so the butler stood between them, his shoulders hunched, his jaw jutting forward threateningly. Miss Frayle gasped in fearful anticipation of what might occur.

'You heard what she said,' the huge man grunted. 'Yer not wanted!'

The Doctor surveyed him calmly. 'I was not aware I was addressing you,' he murmured.

'But I'm addressin' you! Get out, afore I — !'

'Riley!' cut in Mr. Carter, moving towards them, while Miss Frayle hovered uncertainly in the background, goggling nervously from behind her spectacles.

'You do as I say, Riley,' ordered the

woman. 'Clear them out!'

'Yes, madam,' Riley squared up to Doctor Morelle. 'Now then, you want me to throw you out?'

'Oh, Doctor!' cried Miss Frayle.

'Calm yourself, Miss Frayle,' the Doctor reassured her. 'There is not the slightest danger.'

The butler advanced a step, shoving his face close. 'So yer do want to be thrown out?' he rasped.

The Doctor regarded him levelly, his eyes narrowed and piercing. While Miss Frayle watched with bated breath as the man's arm that had been raised threateningly, sank helplessly to his side. Doctor Morelle was speaking slowly in a deadly quiet monotone.

'Riley, your brute strength cannot prevail over my will! As my eyes hold yours . . . So . . . You are experiencing a unique sensation such as you have never felt before . . . Are you not Riley?'

The voice held an extraordinary quality. To Miss Frayle watching open-mouthed, there seemed to be something compelling, mesmeric, about it. The big man's muscles sagged.

'I — I — what's happening?' he mouthed, trying feebly to avoid the steady gaze.

'Riley — what's the matter?' gasped Mrs. Carter, sitting bolt upright, staring at him incredulously.

Doctor Morelle went on in the same monotone while the other stood rooted to the floor. 'Your strength is ebbing away, Riley. You are as weak as a child . . . completely dominated by my will. Are you not?'

'I — I can't move!' he choked in baffled fear. 'Let me go — let me go!'

Doctor Morelle stood with arms folded.

'You may go!' he said, after a moment. The power of movement seemed to return to the man, and he backed hurriedly towards the door.

'Do not hurry,' the Doctor murmured. 'And close the door behind you, quietly.'

His face a mask of amazement and almost pitiful terror, Riley vanished.

No one spoke for a long time. And then:

'Well, I'll be damned!' said Carter softly to himself. Although he had, of course, heard a certain amount about hypnotism and its wider use by the medical profession, this was the first occasion upon which he had witnessed its powers actually being put into operation.

The woman, sitting up in the coffin, however, was by far the most visibly impressed. The amazing episode appealed to her sense of the melodramatic more than anything she had known for a long time. She eyed the Doctor with awesome respect.

'Who are you?' she asked.

'I am Doctor Morelle,' was the studiously simple reply. 'And this is my assistant, Miss Frayle.'

'How — how did you scare him off like that?' she asked.

'Quite simple. So simple I fear it would be far beyond the scope of your comprehension!' He turned abruptly to the husband.

'Mr. Carter, would you be good enough to absent yourself for a brief while? I wish to talk to your wife.'

'Certainly,' agreed Carter willingly. 'I'll be downstairs when you want me.' And with a quizzical glance at his wife he went out. Doctor Morelle drew a chair up to the coffin and waved a hand vaguely to Miss Frayle. 'Sit down, Miss Frayle,' he said.

'Er — there's nowhere for me to sit,' she answered with a look at the chair he was occupying. It was the only one available.

'Then place a cushion on the edge of the coffin,' snapped the Doctor.

She gave a shiver and shook her head. She said:

'I think I'll stand!'

Doctor Morelle turned, clicked his tongue impatiently, and then surveyed the woman in the coffin. He observed she still bore some traces of makeup. Her features, which had once been strikingly handsome, now wore a pudgy, unhealthy appearance. The pupils of her eyes were appreciably dilated.

'Now, Mrs. Carter,' he began firmly, 'tell me, at what time did you learn your child had disappeared?'

At once, her voice reached a hysterical note. 'I was just going to bed — I went to the nursery — and there I found — '

'Answer each question I ask you in as few words as possible,' he interrupted her sharply. The effect was salutary. She became much calmer. 'Now . . . '

'Twelve o'clock,' she told him. 'I heard it striking as I went into the nursery.'

'Have you no nursemaid?'

'She went yesterday morning.'

'You dismissed her?'

'Yes. I didn't like her. I — I felt she wasn't good for the child.'

'Do you suspect her of being involved in the kidnapping?'

'I don't know. She didn't write the note.'

'Note?' the Doctor queried, with a lift of the eyebrows.

'It was left on the pillow. This is it.'

She passed him a sheet of notepaper, on which was typed a message in capital letters. It had been folded across the middle.

'Any envelope?'

She shook her head. He looked at her

keenly, then without a word slowly perused the note. He folded it, tapped it against his fingers, an abstract expression on his face. Then he passed it to Miss Frayle.

Somewhat surprised that he should have noticed she was in the vicinity, she took it. She read:

YORE LITTLE GIRL IS SAFE AS LONG AS YOU DON'T TELL THE POLICE. WE WANT £1,000 FOR HER AND WILL TELEPHONE TODAY AND TELL YOU WERE TO SEND THE CASH. IF YOUVALUE YORE CHILD'S LIFE KEEP QUIET AND DO WHAT WE SAY. — X.

'Do you observe anything significant about this missive?' the Doctor asked as she handed it back to him.

'Yes, Doctor Morelle,' she answered promptly, pleased that he had asked her a question to which she could give an immediate reply. 'Although two or three of the words are misspelled, the actual typing is neat and expert.'

'You fill me with amazement, my dear Miss Frayle! Your powers of observation would appear to be reaching a stage that might be described as almost adolescent!' He went on in an exaggerated tone:

'Do sit on the coffin. You will find it quite comfortable with a cushion on the edge.'

'Very well,' agreed Miss Frayle, gingerly placing a cushion at the extreme foot of the coffin. The Doctor had turned to Mrs. Carter once more.

'You say the nursemaid did not write this?'

'Well, she wasn't illiterate,' she explained.

'I see . . . And you last saw your child, when?'

'At ten o'clock. I looked in the nursery to see if she was asleep.'

'She was sleeping?'

'Yes.'

He nodded thoughtfully.

'Two hours later, however, when you next went to see her, she had gone.' He spoke almost as if to himself. 'So that between the hours of ten and midnight the child was removed. And a note left by the kidnappers . . . '

'Yes! Yes! I was demented!' she cried. 'I didn't know what to do!'

'Quite,' he said.

'The shock was terrible. Terrible!' she moaned.

'How awful for you,' sympathised Miss Frayle.

Doctor Morelle said: 'Your affection for the child is very deep, no doubt?'

'She's all I have in the world!'

'You have your husband,' he gently reminded her.

'Him!' she curled her lips scornfully. 'What does he care for me?'

'That, I feel certain, is a matter for you to decide between yourselves,' he murmured. 'What interests me at the moment is the reason why you prevented him from communicating with me until over an hour after you had discovered the child had gone.'

'I tell you I was out of my mind,' she said desperately. Then added: 'And Riley said I was to leave it to him.'

'I understand,' nodded the Doctor, rising to his feet. 'We must set his and your husband's mind at rest forthwith.'

'What do you mean?' she asked in an astonished voice.

Doctor Morelle regarded her with an air of reassurance.

'Your child is quite safe, Mrs. Carter,' he informed her quietly. 'Furthermore,' he went on smoothly, 'I am confident I shall very shortly be able to ascertain her whereabouts.'

There was a gasp from Miss Frayle, followed by an exclamation of alarm. In her utter amazement at his astonishing statement, she had overbalanced, clutched vainly at thin air for a second, and then subsided into the coffin.

Downstairs, they found Carter restlessly pacing the library.

'That fellow Riley's gone — left no word — ' he greeted them.

'You are well rid of the creature,' said Doctor Morelle.

He nodded. 'I know. The only thing that worries me is whether he may have anything to do with this kidnapping.'

'I very much doubt if he had the intelligence,' said the Doctor. 'No, the person you must seek out if you wish to find the child is the nursemaid your wife discharged yesterday. Rest assured she will not be very far away.' He lit a Le Sphinx and spoke through the cigarette smoke: 'In fact, I should not be greatly surprised if your wife is not aware of her address.'

The other's jaw sagged. 'What — ? What — ?' he gasped. 'You don't mean Bella engineered the kidnapping of her own child?'

The Doctor eyed him keenly.

'Knowing her these past few years as you have done,' he said quietly, 'would that greatly astonish you?'

'I — I — ' Carter was at a loss for words. Then shrugged his shoulders helplessly. 'Perhaps you are right, Doctor. She's behaved very strangely lately.' He set his jaw determinedly. 'I'd better go and have a talk with her.'

Doctor Morelle said: 'That might be advisable at the appropriate moment.' As he and Miss Frayle presently took their leave, he said: 'If you will keep in touch with me, I may be able to advise you as to the precise course of action to pursue.'

Early the following morning Carter was
on the telephone asking for the Doctor.
Miss Frayle stood by expectantly as he
took the call, but his comments in reply
to whatever it was Carter was saying were
characteristically enigmatic. When he had
replaced the receiver she asked: 'They've
found the little girl?'

'Precisely as I anticipated,' he affirmed.
'Mrs. Carter had purposely dismissed the
nursemaid, bribing her to lend her aid in
contriving the bogus kidnapping as a
revenge upon her unfortunate husband
for some imagined grievance. Mrs.
Carter, however, gave away the plot when
she committed a minute but damning
error in the note which purported to have
been left by the kidnappers, but which
she had, in fact, concocted herself.'

Miss Frayle appeared suitably intrigued,
and asked the expectedly appropriate question: 'How was that, Doctor?'

'You may recall Mrs. Carter assured me
the kidnapping had occurred between
the hours of ten p.m. and midnight. Yet

75

the note contained the sentence. 'We will telephone you today and tell you were to send the cash'. Had real kidnappers taken the child, they must have written the note sometime before midnight, and would therefore have used the word 'tomorrow' and not 'today'. Therefore, the implication was that the note had been typed and placed on the pillow after midnight. The logical conclusion to be drawn then was that she was lying, which subsequently proved to be the case.'

'And what's going to happen now, Doctor Morelle?'

'It merely remains for Mrs. Carter to place herself under my treatment. Need I add that in due course her neuroses will be eliminated and she and her husband reunited and the welfare of their child assured?'

'Oh, I am glad you're going to get her right,' Miss Frayle said brightly. Then she smiled; 'But of course you couldn't have allowed her to go on sleeping in that awful coffin!'

His reaction to her remark that was intended to be slightly humorous was typical. He took her perfectly seriously.

'My dear Miss Frayle,' he snapped. 'Why must you pick on a mere side-issue of the case?'

'I'm sorry,' she began, 'I didn't really mean — '

But her apology was too late to repair the damage.

'Will you cease chattering,' he cut in. 'Do you not realise that what Mrs. Carter is suffering from and what I am about to dispose of is a mass of psychological complexes deep-seated in the sub-conscious, and that all outward manifestations . . . '

Miss Frayle sighed, and nerved herself to listen to another profound and lengthy discourse that might have been poured into her ears in the language of Ancient Baghdad for all the sense she could make of it.

# 3

## The Case of the Suspended Foreman

The letter arrived by the morning post. Miss Frayle handed it to the Doctor, together with the rest of the not inconsiderable mail. He glanced at the address with slightly raised eyebrows and then read:

'Dear Doctor Morelle:

I was particularly interested in your article in 'Industrial Science' for this month on the psychological reactions of industrial workers. Judging by your article, I imagine you have been engaged in considerable research upon this subject, and it occurred to me you might find it both profitable and interesting to conduct some practical investigation into conditions at this Power Station.

'When I mention that during the past few months we have suffered two deaths from 'misadventure', you will, I think, agree that there is considerable scope for an investigator of your well-known capabilities, and my company will be pleased to arrange for you to visit us at your earliest convenience. I look forward to your acceptance of the invitation.'

The letter was signed — 'Julian Howard'.

Miss Frayle blinked at Doctor Morelle questioningly.

'Do you think you'll go, Doctor?'

He regarded the letter thoughtfully. Then, tapping it against a thumb, gazed abstractedly over her head. He glanced again at the heading on the notepaper.

'Kindly institute inquiries regarding the locomotive service to Clayford,' he murmured, 'and make the necessary arrangements for our journey to that destination accordingly.'

'Oh, am I coming too?' said Miss Frayle with excitement.

He gazed at her with an expression of sarcastic admiration.

'Your powers of perception are growing more pronounced than ever! Soon, no doubt, I shall be able to converse with you in words of more than one syllable!'

They caught the two o'clock express to the North. They arrived at Clayford just after six. It had started to snow, the station was cavernous and draughty, and a heavy cloud, emanating presumably from the huge chimneys of the power station, hung over the town. Miss Frayle shivered miserably as they drove off in a taxi to the hotel at which they had accommodation reserved for the night.

The hotel, however, gave promise of better things. It was comfortable in an old-fashioned, stolid way, and Doctor Morelle commanded speedy service from the porters, reception staff and waiters with his usual effortless ease. Presently, they were enjoying a substantial dinner, in the middle of which they were interrupted by a thickset man, greying at the temples, who came over to them with profuse apologies for not having met the Doctor at the station. He was Julian Howard. Doctor Morelle introduced him to Miss Frayle, who could not help noting that his suit bulged disgracefully as if his pockets were crammed with blueprints and specifications. He had a blunt, straightforward manner, and there was a vital look in his expression. He seemed to be a man driven by enormous enthusiasm for his work. The Doctor invited him to join them.

'I couldn't get to the station in time,' Howard said, as the waiter placed another chair for him. 'At the last minute there was more trouble in the power station.'

Doctor Morelle gave a sympathetic murmur.

'Another turbine gone west,' Howard went on, 'Benson swears it's foul play, but we can't prove anything.'

'Benson?'

'Our chief engineer. My right-hand man.' He hesitated, then said: 'Can't say I really like the fellow. Never took to him, somehow. Still, I have to admit he knows his job inside out. If he only knew as much about handling men . . .'

The waiter approached and took his order.

Later they moved into the lounge and over coffee Howard unfolded the story he had to tell. Miss Frayle receded into the background and picked up a detective novel she had been reading during the train journey.

According to Julian Howard the trouble had started about a year or so ago. An atmosphere of discontent had begun to pervade the power station. So unobtrusively that it was by no means easy to trace. Benson, it appeared, had not helped matters. His methods were fair but unsympathetic. Then there had been the first fatal accident. After this first death by electrocution, Benson had been heard to say openly on more than one occasion that the workman in question had only himself to blame for starting work on that particular section of cable without making quite certain the current was cut off. He had even declared that if he had been running the firm, the dead man's widow would have received no compensation.

'He's tough,' said Howard, relighting his pipe, which had gone cold. 'But he's got the secret of these new American dynamos better than anybody. Got the knack of knowing just what to do when anything goes wrong.'

'I understand there have so far been two fatal accidents?' Doctor Morelle reminded him.

The other bit on his pipe stem and sighed heavily.

'Yes, I'm afraid so. The second was of a more typical kind. One of the men was caught in a moving belt and dragged into the machinery. Sort of thing that happens somewhere every week.' He paused, then added: 'But there were again some unpleasant repercussions.'

'Indeed?'

'Some of the dead man's fellow workers dropped pretty strong hints that Benson had started up that particular belt before they were ready for it. Of course, it was part of their job to be ready — but they don't look at it that way.'

Doctor Morelle eyed him over his Le Sphinx.

'Your chief engineer seems to be a contributory cause of a certain amount of friction,' he remarked. 'Have you ever considered — ah — dispensing with his services?'

'He has a three years' contract, of which there are about eighteen months to run. He gets big money, pulls his weight, and frankly we can't afford to let him go. We are continually getting new apparatus from America that he understands better than anybody. He was in the States several years.' He shook his head. 'Extraordinary chap! He has the most profound contempt for the working man I've ever come across. I've seen him get livid with rage because some poor devil hasn't quite followed his instructions. Well, of course, the men are apt to bear a grudge. They get their own back in little ways, and that makes Benson wilder than ever. There are times when I think the fellow is not quite right in his mind — but all the same he's Al at his job.'

The Doctor said:

'Is there any unusual feature concerning the home lives of your workmen?'

The other looked at him with some surprise. Then he said, after a moment's reflection:

'Well yes, now you come to mention it, I suppose there is. You see there's no other industry here. Clayford came into existence as a town when we started the Power Station to take advantage of the Pennine streams six years ago. So in their leisure the men don't meet other workers to distract them from their own grievances. I've heard 'em at it, as a matter of fact.' He smiled. 'When they haven't known I've been there, of course!'

Doctor Morelle nodded as if to imply that the other had supplied a clue he had been hinting at.

'What is the gist of their grievances?' he queried.

'Oh, the usual sort of thing — petty interferences, nagging foremen, and so on.'

'Do they refer to this man Benson?'

'Well — he isn't popular. Most of 'em seem to have suffered from his authority — or imagine they have. He's got a lashing tongue, and doesn't hesitate to use it. Some of our skilled electricians are the rather more sensitive type. Don't relish that sort of thing. Of course he can't be solely responsible for this atmosphere of unrest, I suppose. But there's no doubt an unpopular boss can stir up a lot of trouble.'

'That has been my experience in my researches into the subject of the psychological aspect of industrial workers.'

Howard nodded. He went on:

'There was some unpleasantness a couple of months back. Benson apparently took a dislike to a foreman named Gregory. Finally fired him for some petty neglect that resulted in a big transformer being burnt out. According to the men, this was merely an opportunity Benson had been waiting for. They argued Gregory hadn't been responsible for the neglect — it was the duty of one of the under-foremen to check such things, which was true enough. However, we had to back up Benson.'

'With what result?'

'The men staged a lightning strike! Came out for twenty-four hours. We were in a tough spot: our reserves ran right down, and in another couple of hours or so there'd have been no current leaving the station. Of course, under the grid system our load would have been taken over by somebody else, but there'd have been the devil of a fuss. Inquiries and all that. In the end, after a lot of argument, we had to reinstate Gregory.'

He paused to light his pipe again.

'Of course,' he continued, 'we put Gregory on the night shift to keep him out of Benson's way.'

Doctor Morelle smiled bleakly. 'Benson is not responsible for the machines during the night hours?'

'Not officially. He occasionally drops in to see if everything is in order, particularly when there's any new machinery being installed.'

'Your chief engineer seems remarkably interested in his work,' murmured Doctor Morelle dryly.

It was approaching ten o'clock, and, tired after the journey Miss Frayle excused herself and went off to bed. The Doctor and Howard continued their conversation for another hour and then the latter got up to go, explaining with a smile that he made a practice of being in his office never later than eight-thirty each morning.

'Otherwise, I'd never get through half my work! Still, I don't expect you that early,' he added. 'Somewhere about ten-thirty would suit me fine, if that's all right for you?'

The Doctor assured him frigidly that he was himself habitually an early riser, and Howard took his departure.

The snow had ceased to fall, but the Clayford sky was still leaden when Miss Frayle looked through her window the following morning. She shivered and looked forward to their early return to Harley Street.

Over breakfast Doctor Morelle announced that they would walk to the Power Station. The exercise and fresh air would prove beneficial, he declared. Miss Frayle glanced down the dismal street and her heart sank. It couldn't have looked a more uninviting prospect, she thought.

Fortunately, however, a glimpse from the hotel entrance decided the Doctor that the roads were too thick with slush and melting snow, and he abandoned his plan to walk, sending Miss Frayle to order a taxi. They arrived promptly at the agreed time and found Julian Howard busy at his desk. He occupied a very modern office with long steel-framed windows, steel filing cabinets, and an impressive-looking electric light and heat radiation system.

He greeted them genially and pressed a button on his desk. His secretary appeared immediately.

'Ask Mr. Benson if he can come in.'

He turned to Doctor Morelle. 'I thought you might as well meet him right away.' Then, with a grin: 'We always used to reckon to start with the primary causes in the old days!'

From Howard's conversation that she had caught the previous evening, Miss Frayle had expected to see a somewhat large, aggressive individual enter, but Benson proved to be small, and dapper. He was spruce and well groomed with the sleekness of a cat.

'Benson, this is Miss Frayle and Doctor Morelle,' Howard introduced them. 'No doubt you have read some of his articles lately.'

Benson bowed slightly. He smiled at the Doctor:

'Ah yes, the expert in creating happy workers!' And there was only the merest trace of sarcasm in his tone. Doctor Morelle did not permit it to pass unchallenged, however.

'Can it be that my theories have failed to impress you?' he queried suavely. Benson shrugged non-committedly.

'My experiences have been pretty practical,' he emphasised the word rather unnecessarily, Miss Frayle thought. 'And I've always found the men most responsive to strong words and harsh treatment.' He spread his hands. 'Though I understand good results can be obtained by contrary methods. I believe the Maxwell Combine, for instance, have evolved some system: The men have to answer a specially prepared questionnaire amounting to four or five pages: their work is based accordingly. Maxwell's claim it's increased their output twenty per cent. So there may be something in this psychology stuff, but I don't see it working here.'

He glanced at Howard for corroboration. The latter made no comment. Benson showed fine, white teeth in a sceptical smile, and waited for the Doctor to speak. Doctor Morelle assumed an expression of disinterested impartiality that was disarming. It was meant to be.

Howard said: 'Perhaps you'll take the Doctor and Miss Frayle round with you this morning?'

'Sure,' agreed Benson pleasantly. He added, still smiling: 'So long as you haven't got a four-page questionnaire to put to the workers!'

Doctor Morelle permitted himself a thin smile, but his eyes were narrowed and speculative as he and Miss Frayle followed the chief engineer.

They stopped first at Benson's own office, where he pulled a pair of overalls over his suit. 'I sometimes put in a bit of tinkering,' he explained. 'Makes a nasty mess of your clothes — oil dripping all over the place.'

He led the way into a spacious building where the noise of various pieces of machinery merged into a loud humming tone. Doctor Morelle and Miss Frayle followed Benson along alleyways between huge turbines and whirring dynamos.

From time to time the engineer paused to give some instruction or ask a question. The Doctor noticed that on these occasions Benson assumed an unnecessarily harsh manner. The men answered him guardedly, almost sullenly; their attitude was civil, nothing more. Once or twice he climbed over the guarding rail that surrounded the machines and made some small adjustment.

Miss Frayle goggled at the ever-moving machinery from behind her spectacles. She was rather enjoying the sightseeing tour.

'The trouble with the men here is they resent the fact that I know more about their jobs than they do themselves,' Benson told the Doctor.

'Your knowledge is, no doubt, extremely comprehensive?'

'I learned in a hard school,' came the reply.

It was approaching lunchtime when they returned to Howard's office. Doctor Morelle had spent most of the time listening, occasionally asking a question in his characteristically casual way. Miss

Frayle had now become decidedly tired as a result of her traipsing round after the Doctor, and was thankful to sink on to a comfortable settee in the office while Howard, after Benson had quitted the office, talked to Doctor Morelle for a few minutes before they went to lunch.

'Well, what d'you make of him?' asked Howard, eyeing the Doctor hopefully.

'I prefer to reserve my opinion for the time being.' The other smiled.

'All right,' he said. 'If you want to remain mysterious, it's up to you! Anyway let's take it easy for now. Better come and have some lunch.' And he led the way to the directors' room adjoining the canteen.

'Any idea what you want to do this afternoon, Doctor?' Howard asked, as they started their soup. The Doctor glanced at the window.

'I think,' he murmured, 'now that the weather seems a little less inclement, a little exercise is indicated.' And he looked across at Miss Frayle for her approval.

Her heart sank. She had hoped she would be able to return with the Doctor to the hotel and rest after the exertions of the morning. Howard gave Doctor Morelle a sharp glance that indicated he had expected him to devote further time to investigating the cause of the restive atmosphere at the power station.

The Doctor interpreted the other's expression and explained:

'I fear it remains for someone else to make a move before any tangible result can be achieved.'

But even Doctor Morelle could not have foreseen the tragically dramatic nature of that move when it did come.

The Doctor and Miss Frayle were nearing the end of dinner that evening when the waiter hurried in to say he was wanted on the telephone.

The Doctor looked at the man with raised eyebrows.

'Indeed? Who is it waiter, do you know?'

'Gentleman gave the name of Mr. Benson.'

'The chief engineer at the Power Station,' said Miss Frayle helpfully. 'Whatever does he want? I'd better go and see.' A look of slight apprehension crossed her face: she had been anticipating being able to get to bed early, the afternoon's walk had proved as strenuous as the tour round the power station. She felt it in her bones that the telephone message might be disturbing, and her eager offer to answer it was in part a defensive measure. Perhaps she might be able to deal with the menace to her night's rest and nip it in the bud, she thought vaguely.

'Do not disturb yourself, Miss Frayle. I will ascertain the nature of Mr. Benson's requirements.'

'Oh . . . thank you,' she said uncertainly.

Benson's voice was agitated and urgent over the telephone. 'I'm speaking from the Power Station, Doctor. I tried to get our own doctor, but he's not available — I wondered if you'd come over — there's been an accident . . . '

'What precisely has occurred?'

'One of the men has been electrocuted — I'm afraid it's all up with him, poor devil! But I thought perhaps you might — '

'I will come round immediately,'

Doctor Morelle cut in. 'It should take me no more than fifteen minutes to reach you.'

Miss Frayle looked up anxiously as the Doctor returned to the table. He had put on his overcoat and scarf.

'What is it, Doctor Morelle? You look — '

'Benson's up at the Power Station,' he snapped. 'One of the men has been electrocuted. I am going along at once.'

'Electrocuted? How awful! I must come with you — ' He waved her back into her chair.

'No, Miss Frayle, I prefer you to remain here. The weather has turned much too inclement again for you to venture out — '

'Oh, but Doctor — '

'Please take my advice. The wind is icy and I do not wish you to catch a chill. I shall feel much happier in the knowledge that you are here in this more congenial atmosphere.'

His entirely unexpected consideration for her welfare in turn aroused Miss Frayle's protective instincts to the full.

She fixed him with a look much as an astigmatic bird might have devoted to her newly hatched brood.

'Well, if you're sure you'll be all right?' she cooed. 'I don't like you going out alone on a night like this.'

He gave her a sardonic smile.

'I think I shall be able to manage, Miss Frayle!' Then he went on: 'Finish your dinner, and then peruse your detective novel until my return — I feel sure you will find the vicarious thrills therein contained much more gratifying than the comparatively uneventful expedition upon which I am setting out.'

'Wrap up well,' she advised him.

'I will guard myself against the elements to the best of my ability! Expect my return presently.'

'I'll have a hot drink waiting for you when you get back,' she called after him. 'Take care, Doctor . . .'

Outside, it was snowing a little, and as Doctor Morelle came down the hotel steps a taxi drew in to drop its fare. He re-engaged it immediately, with the result that he was passing through the massive entrance gates of the Power Station a few minutes later.

A night watchman directed him to where Benson would be found, and the Doctor hurried off. The chief engineer seemed surprised to see him so soon. He was bending over a figure in blue overalls that lay on a bench.

'You're here quickly!' he remarked. 'It's not a quarter-of-an-hour since I rang you.'

'I said I should come without delay,' replied Doctor Morelle, drawing off his gloves.

'Sorry I had to drag you out on a night like this,' Benson apologised. He added: 'I'm afraid there's nothing you can do.'

'I regret to hear that, Mr. — ah — Benson.' As he bent over the inert figure he said in a conversational tone: 'The wind is immoderately chill. Snow is imminent, I should imagine.'

As he examined the man, a card fell from one of his pockets. It was a club subscription card, bearing the name of John Gregory. As he replaced it the Doctor gave it a cursory glance. At length he stood up.

'Your fears are substantiated,' he told Benson gravely. 'Life is extinct.'

'Not to be surprised at!' was the grim response. 'Ten thousand volts never did anybody much good in a concentrated dose.'

'The cause of death would be compatible with electrocution.'

'I'm a bit puzzled as to how it happened,' muttered the other. 'Though I always said he was damned careless!'

'Perhaps I could view the scene of the accident?' suggested Doctor Morelle.

'See that High Tension wire up there?' He pointed upwards. The wire he indicated was slung from one end of the building to the other, and was about fifteen feet above the ground. 'He was caught on that.'

'You mean, in fact, he was suspended from the wire?'

Benson nodded. 'He must have slipped off that scaffolding you can see runs round the place — as you see we've some structural alterations in progress — '

'You found him there yourself, I presume?'

'Yes — I happened to be checking the instruments, when suddenly they registered a big dip. I came out, had a quick look round, and there was the poor devil!'

'No doubt you promptly switched off the electrical current in this section and extricated the unfortunate man?'

'Yes — had to do it myself, as I thought there might still be a chance, and there was no one else handy to help me. Good job the builders had left those tall steps . . . '

'Then, it seems you were the only witness of this accident to John Gregory?' Doctor Morelle put the question in suave, almost abstract tones.

Benson shot a look at him through narrowed lids.

'What do you know about Gregory?' he said. 'What's on your mind?'

'I am merely suggesting,' murmured the Doctor imperturbably, 'that it was no accident at all. That you have long borne this man a grudge, and that you contrived to electrocute him with malice afore-thought.'

A look of baffled rage showed itself on

the other's face. Then he shrugged his shoulders and revealed his white teeth in a smile.

'You can't prove anything,' he said.

'On the contrary, I shall be in a position when the time comes, to prove as much as is necessary to convict you of homicide.'

'That time'll never come!' grated the chief engineer. As he spoke he produced a revolver and motioned the Doctor back. 'I'll have to give you some of the same medicine!' His face was twisted viciously. 'Back you go . . . Back . . . '

Doctor Morelle gave ground before the menacing figure before him. He realised he was being forced towards a huge condenser.

'You'll fit very snugly between those terminals!' laughed Benson raspingly. 'I'll tell them you were nosing around here — and — well — another unfortunate accident, eh?' He waved his revolver threateningly. 'Back you go, Doctor Morelle! You'll find it a nice quick death — at ten thousand volts!' The Doctor realised that a few more paces would bring about his death. Suddenly he stood his ground. He leaned on his walking stick.

'If you imagine you will escape the consequences of your crime in this way, you are greatly mistaken,' he said in level tones, not taking his eyes from the other's face. 'Before coming here I took the precaution of notifying the police — ' he paused as if listening ' — and unless I am mistaken,' he went on deliberately, 'I am inclined to think I hear their footsteps approaching now — '

The other listened. His eyes shifted craftily as there came the sound of running footsteps drawing nearer.

He made the mistake of turning his head in the direction from which they came. Doctor Morelle's stick struck like lightning to crack against his knuckles. With a shout of pain he dropped the gun. As he clutched his injured hand, Doctor Morelle bent swiftly and now faced him with the revolver. From the door a bewildered Miss Frayle looked questioningly from one to the other, and then came forward hesitantly, her eyes goggling.

'Kindly elevate your hands, Benson,' snapped Doctor Morelle.

'Doctor, what is going on?' asked Miss Frayle in a mystified voice.

'Your appearance was quite fortuitous, Miss Frayle! This — ah — gentleman had taken a pronounced personal dislike to me and had decided to end my career with a violent and somewhat unpleasant death.' His tone changed. 'But I expressly ordered you to stay at the hotel,' he said irritably.

'I — I brought your thick scarf, Doctor,' she stammered. 'You went out with the thin one, and it's started to snow.'

'I feel the scarf would prove more efficacious tied round this creature's wrists! Tie them behind his back, Miss Frayle, firmly.'

Miss Frayle approached Benson nervously, and while the Doctor kept the revolver trained on him menacingly, she followed his instructions. The chief engineer made no sound, but stood there, his face a white twisted mask.

'Don't blame me if you catch a cold,'

Miss Frayle said to Doctor Morelle as she completed her task and stepped back. She went on, surveying the scarf that she had knotted securely round Benson's wrists with approval:

'Thank goodness I felt worried about you! My intuition, I suppose, that you always jeer at! Then when I found your scarf, I had to come after you.' She added brightly: 'Now, would you like me to telephone the police?'

'The manner in which you divine my thoughts is little short of uncanny!' was the reply, and she hurried off.

A little while later Doctor Morelle was saying to Julian Howard:

'I have no doubt but that I have disposed of the source of your anxiety concerning the atmosphere surrounding your employees. Benson was most definitely a sinister influence. Few people are insensitive, consciously or otherwise, to the presence of evil. Its effects upon them are bound to be of a far-reaching nature . . . '

When Howard had gone, Miss Frayle picked up her detective novel and said she thought it was time she went off to bed. She broke off to ask:

'Doctor Morelle, did you say what gave you the clue that Benson was lying about the death of poor Gregory?'

'I should have imagined that would have been apparent, Miss Frayle. Benson's story that he had taken Gregory off the High Tension wire was an obvious fabrication for this simple reason: A person suspended in such a manner would suffer no injury however high the voltage, because the current would not be earthed.'

She looked at him with a puzzled frown.

'But he must have known that too, Doctor, so why did he make up such a story?'

'The creature was of an unbalanced mind, and my speedy arrival at the Power Station upset his calculations and caught him somewhat unprepared.'

She nodded understandingly. She glanced at the book in her hand.

'I must say,' she said, with a little laugh, 'I thought this was quite an exciting story, but after the excitement we've gone through tonight it's going to seem awfully tame!' She paused a moment, and then with the air of one expressing a most profound *bon mot*, observed brightly:

'But then truth *is* stranger than fiction, isn't it, Doctor Morelle?'

# 4

## The Case of the Mysterious Maharanee

Doctor Morelle stepped on to the lecture-platform and surveyed his audience. There were several hundred people present; young intense-looking medical students armed with notebooks; a gratifying number of men who were distinguished members of his own profession. There was also the usual sprinkling of women. These he regarded with his usual somewhat over-elaborate disinterest — until his gaze rested on one whose presence he registered, with an inward feeling of self-satisfaction.

The Maharanee was sitting in her usual place near the door. She had so far attended every lecture in the series, and her continued attendance had intrigued even his curiosity, which was not of the most pressingly obvious kind. Her perfectly chiselled features, jet-black hair and colourful Eastern robes added a distinctive touch to the proceedings. She had, moreover, maintained a mysterious aloofness, never uttering a word even during question time.

Miss Frayle had, of course, been greatly intrigued by the presence of the Maharanee. She had a somewhat old-fashioned notion that all Indian women led a secluded life. She imagined that scientific research would have been quite outside their sphere of activities. The Maharanee, however, and to Miss Frayle's continued interest, seemed to absorb every word Doctor Morelle spoke. She always stayed to the end of the lecture, and seemed to take her leave at the end with some reluctance. She gave the impression on several occasions that she would like to have remained behind to speak to the Doctor.

It was a medical student who happened to sit next to Miss Frayle at one of the lectures who informed her that the woman was a Maharanee. The young man also added that it was rumoured she was in London on some mysterious mission which neither she nor any member of her retinue would divulge. This latter information made her appear even more intriguing in Miss Frayle's eyes, though the Doctor, when she told him what she had heard, discounted the 'mysterious mission' in his usual sardonic way. But then, as she reminded herself, he *would*!

She continued to weave her own idea of the Maharanee's reason for coming to London. She had to admit, nevertheless, that it was difficult to associate anything particularly strange about her regular attendances at the Doctor's lectures. She could only surmise that his own rather odd and mesmeric personality in some way attracted her. Tonight, as Doctor Morelle glanced at his notes preparatory to beginning his lecture she had a seat in the audience from which she could observe the Maharanee closely. She gazed at her now and then through her spectacles, her mind full of conjectures about her.

The Doctor began to speak, and dutifully Miss Frayle forced her gaze and thoughts upon him and his words.

'. . . This evening I propose to deal with some of the rather more obscure poisons of Eastern origin,' he was saying. 'Many of them date back thousands of years, their origins lost in the mists of antiquity, and consequently little is known of them in this country. It is, of course, to be hoped — even perhaps assumed — that it is merely a question of time before our research chemists discover all the true facts concerning all these drugs in question. In the meantime, let us commence with the narcotic group . . .'

Miss Frayle, whose attention had again wandered towards the Maharanee, noticed she had leaned forward slightly in her seat. She seemed particularly attentive to what the Doctor was saying. The intense interest manifest in her grave features, very lovely in their utter repose, did not leave her throughout the time Doctor Morelle was speaking.

When at length he had quitted the platform to the usual demonstration of enthusiastic admiration that he found secretly so gratifying, he retired to a room set aside for that purpose. He was arranging his notes and references in his briefcase, when Miss Frayle appeared. She was very excited and rather breathless. He glanced at her shrewdly.

'While I am aware that my lecture — unique as it undoubtedly was — received a worthily enthusiastic reception,' he commented sardonically, 'I had no idea it would reduce you to this state of extreme agitation!'

Then he noticed she was clutching a folded slip of paper.

'You appear to be the bearer of a communication of some nature,' he said.

'It's for you — from the Maharanee,' she panted. 'It's most mysterious — she gave it to me, very quickly, as she was going out. She didn't say anything — '

He took the note.

'What does it mean?' She goggled at him.

'Apparently an appeal for assistance,' he murmured, without raising his eyes from the message. ''Please come to my help',' he read half to himself. ''I am in

111

great danger. Trust no one. I am surrounded by enemies'.'

'Gracious!' gasped Miss Frayle, clutching at her spectacles agitatedly. 'And she's so young and lovely, too!' She went on breathlessly: 'I found out where she lives — it's just off Park Lane. I believe she's tremendously rich and — '

'What prompted you to learn her address?' He interrupted her with a quizzical look.

'Well — er — ' Miss Frayle hesitated. 'I thought you might want to see her and find out all about this.' She indicated the note he was holding with a vague wave of the hand.

'Why should you assume I might be interested?'

She stammered hesitantly. Then she blurted out:

'Because she's — well, she is very charming — and it's rather romantic.'

'My dear Miss Frayle, are you not becoming somewhat too adult to indulge in dream-fancies usually associated with children's picture books and fairytales?'

'But she never took her eyes off you the

whole time you were lecturing,' she persisted.

'Ah, yes,' he murmured in an irritatingly smug tone of self-satisfaction. 'I thought I spoke exceptionally well tonight. And, of course, a great part of my lecture referred to that part of the world with which she must be familiar.' He lit a cigarette. 'After what you have informed me, Miss Frayle, I feel I can hardly disappoint you! Let us therefore proceed towards Park Lane.'

'We can walk — it's a nice evening,' she said, noticeably excited at the prospect of learning something about the mysterious message and its equally mysterious sender. 'It's not very far.'

'As you wish . . . Ah, yes, I have my walking stick . . . '

They were walking without undue haste through the streets in the vicinity of Curzon Street towards the address Miss Frayle had ascertained, when the Doctor suddenly laid a warning hand on her arm.

'I am distinctly under the impression we are being followed,' he announced in a matter-of-fact tone.

'Oh!' gasped Miss Frayle. 'Followed? But who would it be?'

'I imagine we may ascertain our shadower's identity by slipping into this doorway we are now approaching. Come, Miss Frayle! Quickly and quietly!'

He pulled her into the narrow entrance to a small block of flats. 'Remain motionless,' he ordered in a peremptory whisper. 'In a moment, our curiosity should be satisfied.'

For a few moments all she could hear was the sound of a radio in one of the flats, a dance-band playing a popular tune. Then suddenly she heard very soft footsteps purposefully approaching. She caught her breath as the stealthy tread grew nearer. Then she glimpsed a fleeting picture of the lithe, turbanned figure. Their shadower was almost past them when the Doctor called out:

'Good evening! Were you seeking someone?'

The man stopped dead, turned, and slowly retraced his steps. For a moment he stood watching them warily, his eyes gleaming in his dusky face. Then he spoke:

'You are Doctor Morelle?' he queried in a sing-song tone. 'I have a message for you from the Maharanee.'

'How are you aware of my identity?'

The man appeared not to understand. 'The Maharanee says for me to tell you to forget what she wrote tonight,' he gabbled. 'The Maharanee says for me to tell you all is well now. If you visit her, it would cause trouble for her.'

The man bowed and stood as if awaiting a reply.

'Suppose,' said Doctor Morelle after a pause, 'I am not convinced of the authenticity of your message.'

The man's attitude grew tense, and Miss Frayle, watching his eyes, felt a chill run down her spine.

'I have spoken!' he announced in a menacing tone. 'If you choose to ignore my warning, you may well pay for it with your life!'

'Oh!' gasped Miss Frayle, now beginning to feel thoroughly frightened.

'You understand, Doctor Morelle . . . ?'

'I understand perfectly.' And the Doctor turned to Miss Frayle. 'Miss

Frayle,' he said conversationally, 'you observe that police officer at the street corner? Would you hasten and bring him here at once?'

The man gave a quick exclamation: 'Police!' and muttering unintelligibly, he darted off into the darkness. Doctor Morelle watched him go unperturbed.

'I imagined that might scare you,' she chuckled, as the man vanished into the heavy shadows of some tall buildings along the street.

'There he goes!' cried Miss Frayle, as the speeding figure passed under the light from a street lamp. 'Shall I tell the policeman to go after him?'

'What policeman, my dear Miss Frayle?'

She blinked up at him in owl-like fashion through her spectacles.

'Why — the one you said — the one at the corner.' She turned and scanned the street before them and realised there was no one in sight. She said, puzzled: 'But there isn't a policeman at all — '

He chuckled sardonically. 'Precisely!'

'And — and, there wasn't one?' she stammered.

'The rapidity with which your cerebral tissues operate is positively phenomenal!' he murmured. Then, as if explaining to a child: 'Merely a subterfuge on my part in order to precipitate our native friend's departure.'

'But if you spoke to him in the first place, why did you want to get rid of him?' she asked, still with an air of bewilderment.

He sighed with an expression of long-suffering patience. 'Because I had discovered all he had to tell me,' he said. 'And I did not wish to lose any more time.' He glanced up the street. 'We had better engage this taxi approaching at once. Otherwise I fear I may arrive at our destination too late.'

He hailed the approaching taxicab, which drew up alongside them. He motioned her to step in while he directed the driver.

'Doctor, you don't think anything's happened to the Maharanee, do you?' she asked him anxiously, as they drove off.

'I fear there may be some malignant scheme afoot,' he answered. 'I would

117

hardly describe our recent acquaintance as a friendly native!'

Thirteen was the number of the house outside which the taxi pulled up. It stood in a typical Mayfair thoroughfare, with other large four-storey houses on either side, and was fronted by elaborate ornamental iron railings.

'I hope it won't be unlucky thirteen,' said Miss Frayle in a low voice, catching sight of the number on the door as she followed the Doctor up the front steps. She had hardly spoken when the front door began to open silently, as if operated by a hidden hand.

'Oh!' she gasped. 'It's as if we're expected!'

'No doubt the writer of the missive had some confidence that I should answer it in person,' murmured Doctor Morelle. He paused for a moment, Miss Frayle peering shortsightedly from behind him. The door swung back silently wider. No one appeared to be within. The hall was dimly lit and quiet. An atmosphere of expectancy seemed to grip the house.

'How does the door open by itself?'

Miss Frayle breathed in a puzzled whisper. He made no answer to her question, but moved forward with the remark:

'The invitation extended us to enter could not be more apparent. Follow me, Miss Frayle — and pray do not dig your nails into my arm!' he snapped, as she clutched him in apprehension.

As they stood inside, she looked round to see the door silently close behind them. With a startled gasp she drew the Doctor's attention to this; he murmured impatiently:

'Merely a mechanical device operated by remote control.'

In the dimly lit hall they could discern the outlines of large old-fashioned pieces of furniture. The rugs on which they stepped were thick and luxurious. There was a wide archway with a heavily beaded curtain of Eastern design facing them, and as they were approaching it a gong boomed somewhere beyond it. The gong boomed again reverberatingly. They stood till the last eerie echo had died away.

'Possibly the dinner gong!' suggested

the Doctor with sardonic humour.

'What a heavy scent!' commented Miss Frayle, sniffing. 'It's like incense.' The perfume seemed more overwhelming as they moved forward.

They had almost reached the archway when the curtain was thrust aside with a discordant rattle. An Indian woman appeared with such startling abruptness that for a frightening moment Miss Frayle felt she must have materialised, genie-like, out of the heavy incense that seemed now to engulf them. The woman wore striking Indian robes, and there was the light musical clinking of bangles as she stood there barring their path aggressively.

'Who are you and whom do you seek?' she demanded menacingly. She spoke English with only a slight accent.

'I am Doctor Morelle — ' the Doctor began in level tones, and then turned on Miss Frayle to snap: 'Your fingers are like claws!' Hurriedly, and with an apologetic murmur she withdrew her terrified grasp on his arm.

'I wish to speak to the Maharanee,' he pursued, addressing the woman.

She shook her head deliberately.

'What you ask is impossible.'

'I refuse to believe anything to be impossible,' he answered.

The woman stared at him slowly, her eyes glowing. After a moment's level scrutiny, she spoke and there was a hint of sarcasm in her voice.

'You are no doubt a being of great resourcefulness, great skill, Doctor Morelle — '

He made a deprecating movement.

'But even you,' she went on steadily, 'may not speak to my mistress.'

'May I enquire what is to prevent me?'

'She is dead!'

'Dead!' echoed Miss Frayle in shocked tones.

'She passed away a few minutes ago.'

For a moment no one spoke. Then: 'And the cause of her demise?' asked Doctor Morelle.

'An overdose of Atropine. When the Maharanee returned here she was suffering from a severe headache. She had heard of Atropine for the alleviation of pain, and begged of me to get her some at once from a chemist nearby.'

'And you obeyed her request?'

'No.' Her lips moved as if she was struggling to check her grief. 'Had I done so, this tragedy might not have occurred.'

'What happened?'

'I — I sent one of the servants. When he brought the tablets, I took them to the Maharanee.' She paused. Again it seemed she was overcome with grief and was summoning up all her willpower to prevent her from breaking down completely. 'I — I was called away,' she went on in a low voice. 'When I returned she was dying.'

She wrung her hands in despair.

'Oh, if only she had seen a doctor,' she cried. 'But she never would! She must have taken too much of the drug — '

'Poor woman,' said Miss Frayle in a low voice.

'It would not have been difficult for her to have administered to herself an overdose of the drug,' the Doctor mused. 'The appropriate dose of Atropine is one two-hundredth to one one-hundredth of a grain. One grain might easily prove fatal.'

'Had I been there it would never have happened!' The woman seemed to be able to control her emotion no longer and buried her face in her hands while sobs racked her.

'Doctor, how terrible!' whispered Miss Frayle.

'If you are alluding to her histrionic performance, on the contrary!' he observed shortly. 'She is quite a consummate actress!'

'Doctor Morelle, what do you mean —?'

The woman had ceased sobbing and was staring at the Doctor with a baffled expression. He interrupted Miss Frayle's surprised questioning to address the other:

'If the Maharanee never consulted a doctor in her lifetime, as you have stated,' he snapped grimly, 'it will be necessary for a member of the medical profession to see her now! That is, in the event of your desiring to comply with the demands of the law.'

He paused, his eyes narrowed as he regarded her. Then he said peremptorily: 'Show me to her room without delay.'

'No! No!' She stepped quickly back,

stretching her arms across the archway, as if she would forbid him to pass.

'Very well.' Doctor Morelle's tone was calm and deliberate. 'In which case there will be no alternative but to summon the police.'

He glanced round purposefully in search of a telephone. The woman who had been hesitating now suddenly seemed to make up her mind.

She stood aside, holding the curtains apart, and said over her shoulder: 'Follow me.'

She led the way up a wide staircase, and showed them into a room at the front of the house. It was dimly lit, the atmosphere oppressive. Miss Frayle noticed the Doctor's nostrils quiver suspiciously once or twice as he went across to the bed where the Maharanee lay. Her eyes were closed. An expression of profound repose was upon the finely chiselled features.

Miss Frayle watched him breathlessly as he raised a slender wrist and felt the pulse. Then he bent over the inert form and lifted one of the eyelids. The pupils were contracted. Slowly he rose to his feet.

'Miss Frayle,' he said, without taking his eyes off the figure before him. 'Telephone at once!' He snapped out a number. 'Request them to send an ambulance immediately.' He turned and indicated the telephone at the bedside. Miss Frayle moved forward with alacrity to obey.

'No! No!' cried the woman, stepping forward as if to prevent her reaching the telephone. 'The Maharanee must not leave this house!'

Doctor Morelle turned his level penetrating gaze on her.

Then his voice seemed to crack like a whiplash: 'Those are my orders,' he replied imperturbably. 'You are aware as well as I that the Maharanee is not dead — ! She is merely under the influence of an obscure narcotic of Indian origin known as — .' He mentioned the drug by name.

The woman's whole attitude seemed to sag as the blow struck home.

'Miss Frayle — the telephone!'

The other now suddenly gathered

herself and darted forward as Miss Frayle picked up the receiver. Before she could achieve her object she found herself confronted by Doctor Morelle's tall and dominating figure.

'Remain where you are!' he charged her, his eyes boring into hers. 'My will compels you!'

The woman halted in her stride.

'My will forces you to obey . . . ' his voice was terrifying in its intensity. 'Make no sound, remain quite, quite still!'

She sank into a chair, and remained motionless while Miss Frayle, in a rather unsteady voice, completed the telephone call. Nor did she move again until the ambulance had arrived and the inert form of the Maharanee was borne away upon a stretcher.

'What made you suspicious about that native woman in the first place?' asked Miss Frayle some time later. The Doctor had just returned from the hospital to which the Maharanee had been conveyed with the news that the antidote to the drug had proved effective. The Maharanee was slowly recovering.

He gave her a thin smile. 'I should have thought even you, Miss Frayle, would have realised that the woman's account of how the Atropine was administered was an entire fabrication. No chemist in this country would supply Atropine or any other drug of a poisonous nature without a written prescription from a medical man. The fact that the woman gave no such prescription to the servant who was supposed to have obtained the drug was confirmed later by her statement that the Maharanee had no medical attention.'

He paused to light an inevitable Le Sphinx.

'My suspicions were aroused, however, even before she launched upon that highly fabricated description,' he went on smoothly. 'I happen to know the nearest all-night chemist is situated a mile distant. Even if the servant entrusted with the errand had taken a taxi, it is highly improbable the drug in question would have taken effect so completely within the brief time between the servant's return and our arrival on the scene. Furthermore, when I examined the Maharanee, the contracted condition of the pupils of the eyes was palpable.' He paused theatrically. 'In point of fact, a delirient such as Atropine would enlarge the pupils!'

'You knew she was alive then?'

He shook his head negatively.

'I was not certain. It was very probable that an injection of the drug used by the woman induced a trance of a death-like appearance.' He shrugged his shoulders. 'However, I summoned the ambulance in the hope that this supposition might be correct. Fortunately for the Maharanee, my somewhat speculative diagnosis was proved to be a fact.'

'But — but what was behind it all?'

He puffed a cloud of smoke towards the ceiling. 'I prefer to confine my interest in such matters to the purely scientific.'

'I'm afraid I don't much care for the mystic East either,' Miss Frayle agreed.

'Mystic East my pedal extremity!' was his emphatic reply. 'I could produce all the manifestations you witnessed tonight in my own house now!'

She goggled at him doubtfully. 'Oh,

Doctor,' she said, 'I don't think you could!' His face assumed an expression more saturnine than ever.

'Would you care for demonstrative proof?' he said between his teeth, drawing menacingly closer.

She gasped, terrified by his demeanour.

'Oh, no, no! I believe you,' she stammered hurriedly. And added: 'After all, you did mesmerise that Indian woman in some magical way!'

'Precisely!' he snapped. 'That incident alone establishes my claim that all so-called magic, Eastern or Occidental is explicable. Let us briefly return to that incident which you were pleased to describe as mesmerism. When you were telephoning, Miss Frayle, you may recall that your back was turned to the lady in question.'

'I was so frightened and terrified I wouldn't get the number in time I expect I was preoccupied,' she admitted.

'Your back was towards her,' he snapped with finality. 'But my dear Miss Frayle, had you displayed a trifle more curiosity, you might have observed that she was kept at bay not by my mesmeric powers, but by a thin blade of cold steel!'

'Your swordstick!' she gasped. 'Oh — !'

'And whatever magic powers that woman may have possessed they were of no match for the persuasive powers of my sword — '

And he smiled triumphantly at her and tapped the ash off his cigarette.

# 5

## The Case of the Murdered Artist

During the years of the war against Hitler Doctor Morelle was mainly engaged in important government work, connected with the psychological selection of military personnel for high positions. The set of intelligence tests, designed to show up men of especially high intelligence quotients, which he invented, have for long been considered among the most efficient of their kind. They were, indeed afterwards published in the *International Psychological Journal*, where they attracted considerable attention and were much praised by many of the greatest experts in the world.

Nevertheless the Doctor managed to do a certain amount of work on those criminological themes for which he is more widely known with the general public; although, largely as a result of the shortage of newsprint, he was not given the publicity, which, in pre-war days, had invariably been accorded his exploits of this kind.

One evening during the later stages of the war the Doctor and Miss Frayle were sitting in his study. He was, as usual, dictating; it was, indeed, characteristic of him that he did not allow air raids and all their unpleasant concomitants to move him from his ordinary habits. Miss Frayle was tired and hungry, but, presumably because she had a strong sense of duty and also because she had a wholesome fear of Doctor Morelle's sarcastic tongue, she did not mention to the Doctor either her tiredness or her hunger. Indeed, she went on taking down the exceedingly dull and highly mathematical account of intelligence tests which the Doctor was writing at the request of the American Army authorities, who thought that they might be able to adopt the Morelle system of intelligence tests for their own purposes.

Suddenly, from outside the house,

there came that penetrating wail, which, ever-familiar, nevertheless continued in those days to cause fear and trembling in many households. It was the air raid warning.

'Oh, dear!' Miss Frayle's hand went to her heart and her spectacles slid perilously down her nose.

'My dear Miss Frayle, there is no cause for this inordinate alarm,' the Doctor remonstrated, in what he clearly considered to be reassuring tones.

'But the siren always makes my heart beat fast,' Miss Frayle explained, trying very hard to keep her voice from trembling.

'But surely you have found my explanation of the laws of probability convincing?' the Doctor went on.

'Ye-es.' There was an unwilling sense of disagreement, in spite of the fact that the words indicated agreement with what Doctor Morelle had said.

'And I have explained to you many times that the chances of any individual bomb hitting this house are so small that a reasonable person may safely disregard them,' he continued.

'Ye-es.'

'So I may take it that you will go on with your work and ignore the possible presence of enemy aircraft in the immediate vicinity from now on?' There was a suave sarcasm about the Doctor's voice that did not escape Miss Frayle's attention. She, however, thought it wise merely to say 'Yes' again and to bend her head obediently over her notebook.

She could not refrain from looking at the watch on her wrist, and saying: 'Just seven o'clock, Doctor. Almost exactly the same time as last night.'

'I should have thought,' remarked the Doctor, 'that that was quite a sufficient reason for making your nerves immune from any kind of shock which would in more normal conditions attach to the repetition of that hideous sound.'

It is impossible to say what would have been Miss Frayle's answer to this remark, for at this precise moment the telephone bell rang shrilly.

'Oh, dear!' sighed Miss Frayle, her hand going to her heart once more.

'Really my nerves are getting properly on edge; it might have been a bomb going off.'

'Doctor Morelle's house,' she murmured into the telephone receiver a few moments later, when she had sufficiently recovered to lift it from its hook. 'Oh, yes, Inspector; will you hold on, please?' Miss Frayle turned to the Doctor with an air of suppressed excitement about her. It had, indeed, been some time since she had been enabled to take even a minor part in any kind of criminological investigation, and it now seemed as if something of the sort might be in the offing. She turned to the Doctor.

'It's Inspector Davis, Doctor, and he says that he wants a few words with you,' she explained.

Doctor Morelle grabbed the receiver without more ado. 'Doctor Morelle here, Inspector,' he snapped. 'What? Victor Drayton, the portrait painter, you mean?' There was a pause, during which Miss Frayle waited breathlessly. 'No,' the Doctor then went on, 'he's never been a patient of mine. Why do you ask?' Again there came that pause, during which Miss Frayle could hear the buzz of the Inspector's voice at the other end of the 'phone, though she was unable to hear a word — a fact which she found most tantalizing.

'H'm,' the Doctor resumed. 'And what was the cause of death? Cyanide? I see. And where are you now?'

Miss Frayle shivered; while she never ceased to find cause for satisfaction and excitement over the way in which she had been enabled to work for the Doctor, she nevertheless always felt a little worried and emotionally disturbed over the actual details of the crimes that he investigated.

Now the Doctor turned to her sharply: 'Miss Frayle,' he snapped, 'take this address, please. Victoria Lodge, Victoria Road, North side of Clapham Common.'

'Victoria Lodge, Victoria Road, North side of Clapham Common,' Miss Frayle repeated slowly as she wrote the address down in her notebook.

'Very well,' Doctor Morelle said to his caller, 'I quite understand the position, Inspector. I will come over as soon as possible and see what I can do to help.'

In the darkened streets of wartime London it proved extremely difficult to get a taxi. Miss Frayle shouted shrilly and the Doctor waved his swordstick with tremendous energy; but it was a good ten minutes before they succeeded in persuading a taxi to stop. Once in it, however, it was only a matter of a few minutes longer before they arrived at the Clapham address.

It was difficult to see what sort of house they were visiting; it was, of course, shrouded in darkness, and when they rang the bell it was opened without the least chink of light coming out.

'Inspector Davis?' Doctor Morelle asked.

'Who are you?' came the reply, the owner of the deep voice being, the Doctor thought, a London policeman.

'I am Doctor Morelle,' replied the Doctor in his most impressive tones.

'And I'm Miss Frayle,' that lady added.

'Will you come in, please?' the policeman said. 'The Inspector is waiting for you.'

Miss Frayle blinked as they emerged into a brilliantly lighted room. After the dark streets the light was, indeed, quite dazzling, and it was a matter of some minutes before either the Doctor or Miss Frayle got accustomed to it.

'What's happened?' Miss Frayle asked the Doctor as soon as she had grown accustomed to the new surroundings.

'The Inspector informed me that Victor Drayton, the artist, who lives here, has committed suicide.'

'Oh, dear!' Miss Frayle was alarmed, as usual, at this revelation of what had brought them to Clapham.

'But why have you sent for *us*, Inspector?' she asked.

'There was a note in Drayton's diary, Miss Frayle,' the Inspector said good-humouredly. 'It read: 'Fix appointment with Doctor Morelle. Seems a good man'. So naturally we rang up the Doctor straight away. Thought that he would almost certainly be able to do something to help us in this matter.'

'Naturally,' Doctor Morelle agreed with his usual confidence in himself, 'I shall be able to advise the Inspector here as to the best course of action in these rather awkward circumstances.

'Can you acquaint us with the general circumstances of the case, Inspector?' Doctor Morelle proceeded, when there had been a momentary pause.

'Drayton lived in this house all alone, but for his housekeeper, a woman called Florence Hooper. An elderly woman she is, and, I gather, something in the nature of a poor relation of Drayton, That is, at the moment, about all that I have found out about his personal life in this house.' The Inspector paused, as if he was not quite sure what information the Doctor would find most useful and necessary.

'And the body?' the Doctor asked.

Inspector Davis quietly removed a sheet from a shapeless heap, which had been lying on the floor. 'It has not been touched, Doctor, except to make sure that he was dead,' he said. 'In fact, it is lying just as it was when we found it.'

'Between the easel and this rather beautifully carved old desk,' remarked the Doctor thoughtfully.

Miss Frayle resolutely did not look in the direction of the body, but busied herself by examining the contents of the desk to which the Doctor had drawn attention.

'Looks like a biggish manuscript here, Doctor,' she said. 'A book or something.'

The Doctor picked up the manuscript and examined it with some care.

'Or something is right, Miss Frayle!' exclaimed the Inspector with a grin. 'It's Victor Drayton's autobiography. It seems that he had just finished writing. Some of it's pretty unsavoury stuff to my way of thinking.'

'Oh!' Miss Frayle exclaimed. 'What do you mean, Inspector?'

'Lot of scandal about some of the women he painted,' the Inspector explained apologetically, as if he thought that such matters should not be discussed with a lady.

'But I thought he was only a portrait painter,' said Miss Frayle in puzzled tones. 'I didn't know that he painted them in the . . . '

Doctor Morelle interrupted suddenly. 'I am afraid that Miss Frayle is not exactly sophisticated, Inspector,' he explained, 'and she makes it a little difficult to understand why . . . ' An expressive gesture with his hands made it clear what he meant.

'Sorry,' said the Inspector with another smile.

Doctor Morelle, meanwhile, was examining the studio with some care, as if he thought that somewhere in the room there would be the crucial clue that would lead to the heart of the mystery.

'Bottle of wine on the desk, I see,' he said. 'Chateau Margaux. Half empty. How many wine-glasses did you find here, Inspector?'

'Only one,' the Inspector said.

'Where was it?'

'On the rug. It had fallen down, and didn't break. Had his fingerprints on it. Here it is,' He handed a wineglass to the Doctor, who took it gingerly, raised it to his nose, and sniffed.

'Potassium cyanide,' the Doctor announced. 'No doubt about that at all. Death must have been almost instantaneous. He would die within a few seconds of drinking it.'

While this conversation had been going on, Miss Frayle had been glancing at the manuscript of Victor Drayton's book. Now she looked up from her reading, an expression of intense excitement in her face.

'Doctor Morelle!' she exclaimed.

The Doctor looked at her with a savage smile, 'Yes, Miss Frayle,' he said. 'What momentous discovery are you now longing to announce to us?'

'This manuscript,' she said. 'I've been looking at it.'

'That fact had, strange though it may seem, not escaped my observation,' said the Doctor.

'There's a chapter in it which mentions Florence Hooper,' Miss Frayle announced.

'The housekeeper?' queried the Inspector.

'Yes.'

'And what does it say?' The Inspector, it was obvious, had not yet properly read the manuscript, and was both interested and surprised at what Miss Frayle had discovered.

'It deals with the period when she was a young woman,' Miss Frayle explained, 'I don't think the things he says about her are . . . ' She paused. 'I don't think that they are quite nice — not the sort of thing which a man should put into writing about a lady he's known,' she concluded somewhat tamely.

From outside the room there came what was always one of the most welcome sounds of that time — the sustained note of the 'All clear' siren.

'That's the 'All clear',' the Inspector said somewhat obviously, glancing at his watch as he spoke. 'Just gone eight,' he commented. 'These days a raid always seems to last just about an hour. Almost set your watch by the time they come and the time they go.' He chuckled, and Miss Frayle shivered.

Doctor Morelle did not seem to be at all impressed by these remarks. Indeed, he completely ignored them. He looked at the Inspector thoughtfully.

'Do you think, Inspector, that I might have a word with this Miss Hooper?'

'Yes, of course,' the Inspector said

agreeably. 'I'll get her for you right away, Doctor.' He made his way to the door. Miss Frayle watched him with interested eyes.

'Do you think it *is* really suicide, Doctor?' she asked, as soon as the door had closed behind the Inspector.

'I have so far reached no conclusions, Miss Frayle,' the Doctor announced. 'I am not in the habit of arguing on the basis of data which are obviously fragmentary.'

Miss Frayle smiled a fragile smile, 'If it's . . . ' She paused, as if she found the alternative explanation difficult to put into exact words. 'If it's not suicide,' she said, taking the plunge with alacrity, 'then the housekeeper seems to have what, I think, you would call an adequate motive.'

'Your information is most interesting, Miss Frayle,' the Doctor remarked.

'Thank you, Doctor,' answered Miss Frayle, a blush of pleasure at the unaccustomed compliment spreading across her face.

'I think, however,' the Doctor went on, ignoring her response, 'that you should, if

144

you find it at all possible, refrain from reading any more of that — ah — somewhat highly-coloured literature which seems to form your staple reading matter these days.'

Miss Frayle bridled at this, 'Really, Doctor,' she said, 'I'm not exactly a child, you know.'

The Doctor grinned his usual savage grin at this. 'I am much obliged by your reassurance on that point,' he said. 'I may say, however, that there are moments when I have had some cause for doubt in the matter.'

Miss Frayle tried very hard to think of a satisfactory response to this remark, but found that her brain appeared to refuse to work. It was always so, she found. When she had the opportunity to think the matter over, she remembered a really crushing response; but this seemed always to come to her too late, so that she was never able to utter it at the moment when it would prove genuinely effective. Still, on this occasion she would have no opportunity in any case, since at the moment when she was wracking her brains to think of something, the Inspector returned, bringing with him an elderly woman who was clearly very worried.

'This is Miss Hooper, Doctor Morelle,' he said.

The Doctor nodded gravely.

Miss Hooper spoke in a quavering voice. 'I don't see,' she said, 'what more I can tell you about what's happened tonight. I can't tell you more than what I've already told the police, Doctor, I've given them all the information that I possibly could, you know.'

Doctor Morelle appeared to be singularly unimpressed by Miss Hooper's reassurances. He completely ignored her protestations, and proceeded to question her.

'You were not,' the Doctor began, 'on the premises when the . . . er . . . tragedy occurred?'

'I had gone to the cinema,' Miss Hooper replied.

'You make a habit of doing so?' the Doctor asked.

'Yes. It is my regular day for going, I go

every week, I never miss, and I get home about the same time — seven o'clock. Tonight I came home, just as usual, and I found him, as you know. That is really all that I can tell you about it, Doctor, and, as I said, I told the police all about it before you came.'

Doctor Morelle did not appear especially impressed by this. He did not, however, commit himself in any way, but paused, as if to digest the information, before he asked his next question. That question was: 'You presumably gained admission to the house by the use of your own key, Miss Hooper?'

'Yes,' she replied with an emphatic nod.

'Anyone else besides yourself possess a key to the house?' Doctor Morelle asked quietly, watching her as she thought over the implications of his question.

There was a look of surprise — almost of alarm — in her face as she replied: 'Only Miss Rollo — she's Mr. Drayton's principal model.'

It seemed that there was an air of suspicion about her voice, a suggestion of mistrust of the model whom she had named. Doctor Morelle did not fail to notice it, and he immediately followed up with: 'What sort of person is this Miss Rollo?'

Miss Hooper sniffed superciliously, 'That's a question I wouldn't like to be forced to answer, sir,' she said. 'In here and out, as she likes, at all hours of the day — and night.' Another sniff accompanied the last phrase.

Doctor Morelle again made no comment, 'Only Miss Rollo and yourself had keys, then?' he said.

'And Mr. Drayton himself, of course,' Miss Hooper added, as if it was an afterthought which had suddenly suggested itself to her.

'He would have a key, of course,' Miss Frayle remarked, once more exercising her gift for stating the obvious — a gift which Doctor Morelle always found infinitely irritating.

'Thank you, Miss Frayle,' he now remarked with a bow which was as near as he could allow himself to come to really penetrating sarcasm at Miss Frayle's expense when another woman was present. She was not, however, very conscious of this; and it seemed that Miss Hooper was too concerned with her own affairs to allow herself to be in any way impressed by what the Doctor might say, politely or otherwise, to his amenuensis.

Miss Hooper went on; 'To begin with I didn't know what on earth to do. When I found Mr. Drayton, I mean. Then I realised that it was not something which I could deal with on my own, and that it was my business to 'phone for the police. So I managed to pull myself together somehow, and I went to the 'phone . . . ' Miss Hooper's voice tailed off into silence as she stood and looked at Miss Frayle. It was clear that something had suddenly made her pull herself up with a mental jerk.

She glanced at Miss Frayle with a definite look of apprehension in her expression. Doctor Morelle followed the direction of her eyes with some surprise.

'What . . . ?' she asked and then broke off as if she did not quite know how to frame the question that she had begun: 'What,' she went on, 'has the young lady

149

. . . What have you got there, Miss?' In its final form the question appeared to satisfy her, and she paused and looked at Miss Frayle inquiringly.

'I?' Miss Frayle asked. 'Why, Miss Hooper, I've been looking at this manuscript.'

Miss Hooper seemed to be suddenly speechless. She strode towards Miss Frayle with the nearest approach to genuine resolution that she had yet shown. But, after two or three paces, she paused, as if she was totally unable to make up her mind as to what was the wisest course of action in the circumstances. Then she came to what appeared to be a sudden resolution.

'You've been reading it?' she said in excited tones. 'You had no right to do that — no right at all. Give it to me at once.' There was an almost imperious tone in her voice as she spoke to Miss Frayle, a tone in which that lady, in spite of her unassuming and usually mild ways, intensely resented.

'But . . . Miss Hooper,' expostulated Miss Frayle.

'Give it me, I tell you!' Miss Hooper repeated in the most emphatic tones imaginable.

'Why?' asked Miss Frayle.

'Those horrible lies,' muttered Miss Hooper, 'raking up all that mud from the past. Give it me!' she demanded, more imperiously, even, than before.

The Inspector obviously thought that it was high time he took a hand in the argument. 'Now, now,' he said quietly, 'Take it easy, Miss Hooper. Don't get over-excited, now. Whatever there may be in that book won't do you any harm, and I'm sure that Miss Frayle had no intention of prying into anything that didn't concern her.'

'That is as it may be,' Miss Hooper objected. Whatever else she was going to say was lost to them, as at that moment the outer doorbell jangled, making them all, in their somewhat highly-wrought condition, suddenly start as if they had been detected in the committing of some crime.

'Who's that?' Miss Hooper exclaimed — the first one of them to show any definite reaction to what had happened. 'That's someone at the door. Who can it be?'

The Inspector again tried to soothe her. 'My sergeant will answer it, Miss Hooper,' he said quietly. 'There's no need for you to get alarmed. Just you sit down and try to answer Doctor Morelle's questions.'

Miss Frayle looked at the distraught woman with real pity. She was sure that Miss Hooper was alarmed quite unnecessarily. 'Yes, Miss Hooper,' she said in the most sympathetic voice that she could command. 'Really, I'm quite certain that whatever has been written about you here,' — she pointed to the manuscript which she had been studying — 'won't be allowed to come out in public and won't be allowed to hurt you at all.'

It was impossible to say what was Miss Hooper's reaction to this remark, since the door suddenly burst open and a strange woman came in. She was dressed in an exotic dress, with oddly contrasting colours and curious trappings, including rings and bangles, which suggested the gypsy more than any kind of national characteristic. Miss Frayle, gazing open-mouthed, thought that she had never seen such a strange character.

'Where,' asked the newcomer in a foreign accent, 'is Victor? What has happened to him? What is the matter? Will someone kindly tell me?' Indeed, she looked most distraught at what was going on, as if she was absolutely mystified but at the same time very worried.

'My name is Nita Rollo,' she said.

'Oh!' Miss Frayle gasped, looking at the woman with the greatest interest.

'I am a model,' she explained. 'I was Victor Drayton's usual model for years. But . . . ' She hesitated.

'But what, Miss Rollo?' asked Doctor Morelle quietly, as if he anticipated some strange response.

'But . . . but . . . why are the police here?' she asked. Then a look of sudden horror came into her eyes. 'Victor!' she screamed. 'He's done it! He's . . . oh, Victor!'

The inspector looked at her curiously.

'What do you mean by that. Miss Rollo?' he asked.

'By what?'

'By 'He's done it',' explained the Inspector. 'What do *you* know about Victor Drayton's death?'

Nita Rollo looked thoroughly depressed — even broken by this confirmation that Drayton was, indeed, dead.

'He has been very depressed for a long time,' she said.

'Why?' the Inspector snapped out.

'Because of his painting. He said that it was in some way deteriorating. He had threatened to kill himself, for he said that he was losing his skill, and that soon his paintings would not be any longer saleable.'

'I see.' The Inspector looked thoughtful at this. It seemed that he found real food for thought in what the model had to tell him.

'It is because of his depression that I have been away for a time,' Nita Rollo explained. 'He thought that he would stop working for a while and give himself a rest. Then he would get over his staleness.'

Doctor Morelle had been very quiet while this discussion was going on, taking no part in the conversation, but watching Nita Rollo very carefully, as if he thought that a study of her face might bring him some special revelation as to what had gone on.

Now, however, he interposed a sudden question. 'You have been away?' he asked.

'Yes.'

'Out of London?'

'Yes,' she said. 'But I did not get from him the letters I had been expecting. I felt very uneasy about him, and so I came back to see if he was all right. I arrived at Euston at 7.35. I had a sort of presentiment that he was in real danger and so I came here as quickly as I could by tube.'

The Inspector appeared to feel a trifle suspicious at this explanation. Possibly he felt that it was a little too well thought-out to be true. At all events, it seemed that he wanted some confirmation before he was prepared to accept it at its face value.

'Miss Hooper,' he said, 'can you

positively identify this lady?'

'Yes, sir,' answered Miss Hooper without a trace of hesitation. 'She is Mr. Drayton's model all right. I expect that you will find that she is dealt with in some detail in his book, too!'

Nita Rollo seemed to be a little taken aback by this remark, which had clearly been quite unexpected by her.

'You mean,' she said, 'the life story — autobiography — that he was writing?'

'Yes.'

'It's on the desk here,' Miss Frayle put in, since she had not asked any questions, not in any way contributed to the discussion for some time. As usual, she felt that she must put a spoke in now and then, if only to justify her position as Doctor Morelle's secretary and amenuensis.

'It ought to be burned!' exclaimed Miss Hooper with considerable emphasis.

Miss Rollo smiled. 'I imagine that there are a good many women who would agree with you there, my dear,' she said quietly. 'Not that I, personally, care about what Victor said about me. But it might be the sort of book which would upset some people, of course.' There was a world of meaning in the tone in which the last phrase was spoken.

'I understand,' snapped Doctor Morelle, 'that you were able to admit yourself to this house at any time which you desired?'

There was some slight hesitation about Nita Rollo's reply to this question, as if she saw that there was some ambiguity about the fact.

'Yes, I had my own key,' she admitted. 'I'd often be called in to work for Mr. Drayton at odd hours,' she explained somewhat defensively. 'And as a result it was a matter of convenience that he should let me have a latchkey to let myself in with.'

Doctor Morelle nodded, as if he accepted this as reasonable enough. The Inspector coughed warningly, thinking that it was high time the discussion was taken back to its proper lines.

'This life-story book, Doctor,' he said, 'seems to be a bit mixed up with the whole business, if you ask me.'

'You think so?' Doctor Morelle's expression was completely non-committal.

'Yes. And what's more I feel that there is a lot more in this case than meets the eye. I don't believe it's quite so much an open-and-shut business as we thought it was to begin with.'

'Indeed, Inspector?' There was almost a twinkle of humour in Doctor Morelle's eye now.

'In fact,' the Inspector went on, 'I'm not so sure now that we can altogether rule out the possibility of foul play, Doctor.'

This brought real amazement to Miss Frayle who had listened to these remarks with eyes opening wider and wider.

'Inspector!' she exclaimed. 'Surely you cannot mean to say that this is, after all. a case . . . a case . . . a case of . . . ' She paused. 'That there has been foul play,' she concluded somewhat lamely.

Doctor Morelle held up his hand, and smiled in his usual sardonic fashion.

'I believe that you know something about what has been going on, Doctor!' she exclaimed.

'The Inspector said that it was a possibility that there had been some foul play,' the Doctor said. 'I myself should have said that it had been established with complete certainty that the deceased was murdered!'

In her time Miss Frayle had had more than one surprise in connection with Doctor Morelle and his criminological deductions. It was a long time since she had first started work with him; but it was probable that this occasion was the most surprising of them all. She just gasped and stared; the suggestion that, in spite of the external appearances of suicide, this was a case of murder, gave her the greatest thrill which she had felt for many a long day, and she waited breathlessly for the revelation which she was sure would be soon forthcoming.

It was, however, not to be vouchsafed to her to understand for some time just what had happened. She was therefore annoyed that Doctor Morelle, at this exciting moment, insisted on her leaving the room. Indeed, he more or less pushed her out of the room, It was one of the most humiliating experiences of her life, And she had to wait before the Doctor came out, and, without a word, escorted her to a taxi and so back to his house, before she could find out what had happened.

'Who is the murderer, Doctor?' she asked when they were in the taxi.

'I shall have to ask to restrain your impatience, Miss Frayle,' Doctor Morelle said quietly. 'When we get back to the study I will proceed to dictate to you the essential points on this case. Then it is possible that some matters which at the moment mystify you, will become abundantly clear.'

When they reached the study Miss Frayle was more and more impatient and excited. She knew that the Doctor had some really surprising news to communicate; but she also knew that nothing that she did would really make any influence with him in the matter.

'It was,' he said, when they were ensconced in the study, Miss Frayle with her notebook open and her pencil poised above a blank page, 'obvious to the meanest intelligence that Victor Drayton had been poisoned by his model, Nita Rollo.'

The Doctor paused. Miss Frayle looked more than a trifle hurt. 'If that's a dig at me, suggesting that I've got the meanest intelligence, I don't think it's very generous of you, Doctor!' she exclaimed.

'My dear Miss Frayle,' the Doctor returned, 'you are putting words into my mouth.'

Miss Frayle smiled. 'That would be carrying coals to Newcastle,' she murmured; but the murmur was sufficiently subdued for it not to reach the Doctor's ears,

The Doctor went on: 'I first suspected the Rollo creature when she rang the bell in order to gain admission to the house. You will of course recall that she did so.'

'But what is suspicious about that, Doctor?' asked Miss Frayle in surprised tones,

'I should naturally have expected her to make her entry with her latchkey in the usual manner,' the Doctor explained.

'And had she now known that such a mode of entry would be likely to arouse our suspicion, she would doubtless have used it.'

'But she admitted that the key was in her possession,' Miss Frayle objected.

'Yes,' agreed the Doctor. 'But only when she realised that I knew she had a key. She was then forced to admit it immediately, and she thought that it was safer to do so without any kind of arguments. But had she not thought that she might be in jeopardy, she would never have admitted the possession of the key.'

'And when she admitted it, she hoped that no one would remember that she had rung the bell just before?' Miss Frayle said.

'Precisely,' Doctor Morelle said with a smirk of satisfaction 'Furthermore, she lied in her statement relating how she had travelled by Underground from Euston . . . '

'But she had plenty of time to get to Clapham,' Miss Frayle said. 'Her train got in at Euston at 7.35, and she reached us just after eight o'clock . . . '

Doctor Morelle held up his hand imperiously, 'I should have imagined,' he said, 'that anyone residing in London during the international conflict would know well enough that Euston lies on the north side of the river Thames and Clapham on the south side. And during an Air Raid alert, such as was in operation, you will remember, while we were at Victor Drayton's studio, the tunnels under the river have always been closed.'

'Of course!' exclaimed Miss Frayle. 'South-bound trains are stopped at the Bank, and north-bound trains don't go further than London Bridge station. And those conditions go on until the 'All-clear' is sounded.'

'You will remember that the 'alert' sounded before 7.30, and that the 'all clear' didn't go until approximately eight o'clock,' the Doctor said. 'If she had been travelling by Underground at that time, as she stated, she would have been held up by the air raid warning for at least half an hour, and it would therefore have been totally impossible for her to have reached

Clapham by eight.'

'But why did she do it?' Miss Frayle inquired.

'When she was arrested by the Inspector she broke down,' the Doctor said. 'I sent you out of the room because I feared that there might be a thoroughly unpleasant scene.'

Miss Frayle smiled. 'I am very grateful, of course, for your thoroughness, Doctor,' she said. 'But at the same time I should like to know what it was all about.'

'It came out,' said the Doctor, 'that Drayton had broken off his association with Miss Rollo, and she — a jealous and passionate type — refused to be flung aside in that way, and murdered him. A woman scorned, Miss Frayle . . . '

Miss Frayle smiled. 'I know, Doctor!' she exclaimed. 'Or do I? Anyhow, here is a woman hungry! I think that we could have something to eat, don't you?'

# 6

## The Case of the Anonymous Postcards

Doctor Morelle regards the strange happenings at Bleakcliff as perhaps the most unique of all the cases he has investigated. True, he is not accustomed to understatement in his description of the mysteries he has solved, any more than he is inclined to underestimate his own peculiar powers of deduction and ratiocination.

One reason, however, for his high estimation of this particular case as a tour de force among his catalogue of criminological successes is admittedly justifiable. It is the fact that an outstanding feature of the case was the complete absence, in any material sense, of any clue.

Nevertheless the Doctor's elucidation of the mystery was achieved by his extraordinary aptitude to grasp the essential facts, logically to arrange them so that they presented a true picture of the actualities. Added to these undeniable gifts was his shrewd and penetrating insight into the human mind. To him, it seemed, all the processes however secret, however twisted and subterranean, of the human intellect were laid bare for his dissection at his will.

Bleakcliff has always steadfastly refused to be classified as a holiday resort, though it occupies a pleasant position on the edge of the Thames Estuary. Little more than a village with perhaps a dozen shops in its narrow High Street, it is well off the beaten track between London and the East Coast popular resorts so favoured by the holiday making multitudes. Bleakcliff offers no attractions apart from its bracing air, its well-ordered countryside, surprisingly unsullied in the immediate vicinity by petrol pumps or cheap building enterprises. In fact, there are very few new houses in the district, chiefly owing to the fact that local authority frowns in no uncertain manner upon anything which might in any way endanger the quiet, attractive rural atmosphere. Faced with such a backward and unimaginative attitude, the two local building contractors have long since transferred their activities to more go-ahead and remunerative fields.

Doctor Morelle had recommended the tonic qualities of Bleakcliff to Arthur Hall, when he was treating him for after-effects of a motor accident, which had exacted a heavy toll on his nervous system. His case had proved responsive to the Doctor's treatment. After only a few visits to the charming house his patient had been fortunate enough to secure at Bleakcliff, Doctor Morelle considered the man had adjusted himself satisfactorily to a new life and his services were required no longer.

Hall and his wife settled down to become highly respected residents, living a staid, unexciting life. The neuroses that had affected Hall as a result of his accident gradually faded into the background of his mind like the remnants of half-forgotten evil dreams. He could not imagine that he had ever endured such sufferings of the mind and spirit, so far removed were they now, so dim and hazy were their memory. Life had become a gentle flow of incident and interest as unruffled and unhurried as a slow, quiet stream. And then evil disturbed the peace and contentment, not only of Hall's placid life but the lives and uneventful happiness of other residents of Bleakcliff.

Doctor Morelle had, not unnaturally, in the course of his subsequent busy career almost forgotten Hall's existence. He was somewhat surprised one morning to receive a letter from the husband stating that his wife was very ill, and that he would take it as a great favour if the Doctor would pay them a visit as soon as possible.

As it happened, Doctor Morelle had just concluded a spell of intensive laboratory experiments, and the two hours' drive by car to Bleakcliff appealed to him as a very welcome break. Miss Frayle was even more eager and delighted at the prospect of a drive to the coast. She had spent the last few days in the laboratory taking copious notes of names she found difficulty in spelling, and endeavouring to simulate an interest in a series of chemical processes which appeared to her singularly intricate and difficult to comprehend.

They found Bleakcliff very little altered from the Doctor's memory of his last visit some years previously. The stately Victorian houses still edged the High Street. The little shops still dressed their windows in a style that had long gone out of fashion in the chromium-plated shops of the sophisticated large towns.

'It would be rather nice to retire and live here, wouldn't it, Doctor?' suggested Miss Frayle brightly, as they drove up the short drive in front of the Halls' house.

'So far as I am concerned, retirement suggests two provisos — failing physical health and decaying brain tissue,' he replied acidly. 'At the moment, I possess neither one nor the other!'

He brought the car to a standstill. As he did so the front door opened and Arthur Hall came running down the front steps to greet them.

'I'm so glad you could get here,

Doctor,' and there was relief and hope shining plainly in his eyes.

'This is my assistant, Miss Frayle, who occasionally assists me in my work,' said Doctor Morelle, sardonically ambiguous. Hall ushered them into a cheerful sitting room, and ordered tea to be brought in at once. While it was being served he gave a description of the illness that had struck at his wife. When he had finished his story the Doctor asked to see Mrs. Hall right away.

'I'm afraid she's very upset, Doctor. She may not answer your questions.' He went on, his face worried and puzzled: 'You remember what a cheerful sort of person she used to be?'

Doctor Morelle nodded: 'Her good spirits were of great assistance in effecting a cure in your own case.'

'That's true . . . well I'm afraid you'll find she's changed. Since she went to bed four days ago, she's refused to get up. Hardly speaks to anyone. As I've told you, she thinks she's being spied upon — '

'A common hallucination in such cases,' the Doctor informed him as they went into the hall, leaving Miss Frayle to continue her tea. They were away nearly half-an-hour, and when they returned Doctor Morelle appeared thoughtful. He took a Le Sphinx from his case and lit it. Hall, his eyes dark with anxiety, filled an old pipe.

'There would seem to be a somewhat obscure reason for Mrs. Hall's illness,' murmured Doctor Morelle. He turned to the other: 'Have you no clue as to what may have been responsible for her suddenly retiring to bed suffering apparently from nervous collapse?'

Hall was silent for a moment, then slowly took a wallet from his inside pocket and extracted a postcard. 'I didn't mention it at first,' he said. 'I didn't quite know whether you ought to be told, or the police. I — I felt perhaps I ought not to worry you with it, that it hadn't really got anything to do with my wife being ill like this — '

Miss Frayle saw Doctor Morelle take the postcard with ill-concealed impatience.

Hall went on: 'It arrived the morning my wife collapsed. She saw it before I could intercept it. That card is the cause of all the trouble, I feel it in my bones, but I — I don't know . . . you may think it's nothing — just a practical joke or something . . . ' his voice trailed off.

Doctor Morelle read:

'YOUR CONSCIENCE MUST BE AROUSED. EXPIATE YOUR CRIME OR THE POLICE WILL BE INFORMED. THE VOICE OF YOUR GUILT WILL NOT BE SILENCED.' It was written by hand in neat block capitals, and addressed to Mrs. Hall.

'Obviously,' he snapped,' this is a contributory cause of your wife's breakdown.'

'It must have been dropped through the letterbox either late at night or early in the morning.'

'I had already assumed that it was not delivered through the post.'

'Why?' asked Miss Frayle, somewhat unthinkingly.

'Because,' said Doctor Morelle, 'I had observed the absence of any postage stamp!' Hall seemed about to speak, then hesitated.

'You have no idea who might be the perpetrator of this hardly innocent little missive?' the Doctor asked.

The other shook his head.

'All I know is that several others in Bleakcliff have received these poison-pen cards.'

'Indeed?' The Doctor gave him a narrowed look.

'What a beastly thing to do!' exclaimed Miss Frayle.

'I don't know if the police are trying to trace the writer,' added Hall.

'They would have a somewhat difficult task,' was Doctor Morelle's comment. 'However, with my assistance they should in this case succeed.'

Hall looked at him quickly, a surprised expression momentarily creasing the worried frown:

'I had no idea, Doctor, that you interested yourself in — ?' he broke off.

'Criminal investigation?' the Doctor smiled a smile of somewhat over-elaborate deprecation.

'Didn't you read his evidence in the Mayfair Poisoning Case?' asked Miss

Frayle. 'Oh, it was most interesting!'

'Thank you, Miss Frayle!' murmured the Doctor sardonically.

'I — er — I'm afraid I don't read court cases,' Hall admitted, obviously embarrassed at his ignorance of Doctor Morelle's eminence in criminological matters.

'Indeed?' The Doctor regarded him with an interest somewhat similar to that he might have shown on encountering for the first time a sample of bacteriological evidence hitherto unknown to him. He gave a slight cough. 'However, no doubt you are familiar with the whereabouts of the local Police Station?'

'Why yes. It's at the other end of the village — opposite the Post Office.'

'Are we going there, Doctor?' asked Miss Frayle with a little anxious frown, noting him pick up his hat and gloves. He turned to her with the merest flicker of a smile.

'Be not afraid, my dear Miss Frayle, they won't need your fingerprints — ' and added as if as an afterthought: 'Yet!'

'Would you like me to come with you?'

suggested Hall rather helpfully. 'Perhaps I could — er — explain — who you are — ' he broke off vaguely.

'That will not be necessary,' the Doctor reassured him. 'I imagine my name might be familiar even to a village constable — no doubt they have access to the daily newspapers here! Come, Miss Frayle, let us call upon the rural constabulary . . .'

'I believe one of the officers is named Preedy — er — Sergeant Preedy,' Hall said to him as they went into the hall. Leaving the car outside the house, he made his way, followed by Miss Frayle towards the village. It was early evening, drowsy after a long, fine summer's day, and there were few signs of activity. One or two cars passed them; in them middle-aged ladies who appeared as if they might be on their way to pay calls upon their fellow residents. The atmosphere of the High Street was rather reminiscent of a miniature edition of Bath or Cheltenham.

They had no difficulty in finding the Police Station. It was a fairly large Victorian building with an imposing front

175

entrance marred somewhat by its notice board, overflowing with a varied collection of announcements. Most of them appeared to be concerned more with agricultural than criminal matters.

Sergeant Preedy himself answered the Doctor's ring. Upon learning his visitors' identities he welcomed the Doctor and Miss Frayle with eager interest. He very rarely saw a new face in the district, let alone visitors from London — and the arrival of such distinguished personalities as he was now entertaining was an event of unprecedented importance! Preedy, despite his bucolic countenance, was by no means the yokel policeman so often burlesqued on screen and stage.

He ushered them into a large room that had been converted to the purpose of an office. The walls were generously plastered with the same posters and notices that were exhibited outside. Two policemen's helmets hung behind the door. He said with suitable deference:

'Well, Doctor Morelle, what can I do for you? What's the trouble?'

'I imagine it is conceivably your

trouble, too, Sergeant,' the Doctor replied smoothly. 'Briefly, it concerns these anonymous postcards, a number of which I understand have been delivered in the village.' A worried look immediately appeared on Sergeant Preedy's pleasant face. He pulled open a drawer in a big desk by the window.

'Like this?' he asked.

Doctor Morelle took the postcard the other handed to him and examined it. It was an exact duplicate of that addressed to Mrs. Hall, but was in this case addressed to a Mr. Barwell.

'Nothing to go on, you see,' said Preedy. 'Nothing. And that's the trouble.'

Miss Frayle glanced at his troubled expression and back to the Doctor who said:

'Merely these postcards, each with precisely the same message? And delivered in a like manner?'

'Seven of 'em in all.'

'Eight, including Mrs. Hall,' murmured the Doctor.

Sergeant Preedy stared at him. 'Mrs. Hall — is she another one?'

The Doctor nodded.

'Poor woman, it's upset her terribly,' put in Miss Frayle, 'How can people be so cruel?'

'How did you know about it?' asked the other, scratching his grey head in perplexity.

'Mr. Hall happens to have been a patient of mine,' explained Doctor Morelle. 'When his wife received this postcard the shock affected her and she is now on the verge of a nervous collapse.'

'I see.' He glanced at the postcard the Doctor had returned to him and rubbed his chin thoughtfully.

'I wish the people who get these wouldn't take 'em so seriously,' he ruminated. 'It's just what the person who sent 'em wants!'

'The recipients are prominent persons locally it would seem?'

'Oh yes, bigwigs of the neighbourhood. Think a lot o' themselves they do!' He grinned tolerantly at Miss Frayle. 'Come and tell me all about it in a proper fluster that anybody should dare to insinuate they were mixed up in anything not quite above-board.' He chuckled reminiscently. 'I've told one or two of 'em that a man who's never broken the law in some way or other must have spent his life in a monastery or something like it! Be surprised how that makes 'em stop and think.'

Miss Frayle gave him a little smile conveying approval.

'All the same,' he continued, 'it's a worrying business. Especially with rumours beginning to get about. You know how these people are, Doctor Morelle. When they're up against something a bit out of the ordinary. Lot of scared hens!'

Doctor Morelle nodded. He offered no comment.

'Had a couple of silly old spinsters in here this morning. Insisted, if you please, I should go and arrest Miss Lang up at Bleak Priory.'

'Miss Lang?'

Sergeant Preedy rubbed his chin again. 'Queer old girl who lives at Bleak Priory. Been here years, writing a book on the locality — that's why they say she knows everything about everybody.'

179

'She sounds as if she might, don't you think?' put in Miss Frayle tentatively.

Preedy shrugged non-committedly. 'Anyone, for that matter, who's been in Bleakcliff any length of time, can find out all there is to find out about the other inhabitants. Yes. Got nothing else to do but gossip and tittle-tattle.'

'Nevertheless, I should care to converse with this Miss Lang.'

'If she'll let you, Doctor Morelle!' the other returned.

'You feel she may object?'

'Try her and see!' Sergeant Preedy's attitude implied the Doctor would be wasting his time.

'That is exactly what I propose to do!' Doctor Morelle ignored the implication. 'Bleak Priory, did you say is her place of residence?'

'That's right, Doctor. Stands on the hill at the back here.' He pointed through the window. 'You can't miss it. Turn left at the crossroads. They say monks lived there about five hundred years ago, and it's undermined with secret passages. Cosy little corner — I don't think!'

However, this somewhat sinister description was entirely wasted upon the Doctor. Informing the Sergeant he would advise him in the event of his discovering anything, he set off in the direction indicated at a brisk pace. Miss Frayle hurried along after him, being forced to make strenuous efforts to keep up with his long strides. The sky had suddenly become overcast and clouded. A chilly northeast wind was whistling through the trees as they came into sight of the Priory. It was a gaunt and black-looking building, standing on the side of a hill, as Sergeant Preedy had told them. As they approached it, however, it became evident that it was in an uninhabitable condition. They paused for a moment to survey the place.

'Do you think this can be the place, Doctor?' asked Miss Frayle doubtfully.

'According to Sergeant Preedy's directions, it would appear so.'

'But it's an old ruin.'

And indeed, most of the walls were crumbling, and several of them had been reduced to nothing more than heaps of stones. Masses of dark ivy crawled over the derelict mass.

'The fading light obscures one's vision, but the building does present a somewhat derelict appearance,' conceded the Doctor, as they drew slowly nearer. 'Possibly, however, there are habitable quarters in the regions at the back.'

They walked through towering entrance gates, which swung rusted and creaking on massive pillars. The moss-patched and weedy gravel path crunched under their feet as they approached the wide porch. The wind whistled dismally through the broken windows and crevices in the stonework. Bats fluttered silently over their heads. Somewhere an owl hooted.

Miss Frayle could not suppress a shiver as the wind moaned more loudly round a corner.

'Just listen to the wind!' She spoke in a whisper, as if in danger of being overheard.

'Miss Lang would obviously appear to be a devotee of the fresh air cult!' was Doctor Morelle's comment.

Miss Frayle suddenly clutched his arm. 'Listen!'

They listened intently. Very faintly, came the sound of a stick tapping upon worn flagstones. In a moment the heavy door before them creaked open and a strange figure presented itself in the doorway. A long grey cloak was thrown over her shoulders; her white hair fluttered in the gusts of wind.

'Go away!' the apparition screeched. 'Go away!'

'Miss Lang!' breathed Miss Frayle.

'No doubt she would answer Sergeant Preedy's description!' murmured Doctor Morelle.

Apprehensively she clutched his arm more desperately than ever. Miss Lang came nearer and waved a thick, heavy stick threateningly. Her eyes were hidden by tinted spectacles that gave her an even more forbidding appearance.

'Oh Doctor — she's terrifying — those dark glasses — !' Miss Frayle gulped.

'I know what you've come to find out, but I won't answer,' called Miss Lang hysterically. 'Go away — I won't answer!'

Although Miss Frayle was dragging at his arm, urging him to move, the Doctor stood his ground. The advancing woman halted a few feet away.

'You've no reason to suspect me any more than the others in Bleakcliff,' she shrilled.

'Why, Miss Lang?' asked Doctor Morelle, calmly and quietly formidable.

Miss Frayle imagined she saw the eyes flash behind the dark glasses.

'Because there are no secrets in this village! Everyone spies on their neighbours!'

'Have they discovered the particular skeleton that rattles in your cupboard?' the Doctor queried in an insinuating voice. The thrust seemed to find its mark.

'Go away!' Miss Lang was advancing on them again, her voice discordant and cracked with fury. She waved her stick with increasing menace. 'Strangers aren't welcome here! Away!'

'She'll attack us!' cried Miss Frayle, now thoroughly frightened.

The wrath seemed to be about to burst over them. It was too much for her. Letting go the Doctor's arm, she ran for dear life the way she had come.

Miss Lang came almost within striking distance of Doctor Morelle, her stick raised threateningly.

'Be advised and follow her — go!'

He shrugged resignedly.

'Since there would seem little to be gained by remaining, I will accept your advice.' Turning abruptly on his heel, he murmured, elaborately polite: 'Good evening, Miss Lang!'

'Good riddance!' she flung after him. He heard the tapping of her stick retreating back the way she had come until it was caught in the howling of the wind.

He made his way unhurriedly through the gates. Outside he stood for a few moments to turn back and survey the desolate scene in the growing dusk. The woman had disappeared into the crumbling mass of stone and ivy. Suddenly, he imagined he heard a muffled cry for help. It appeared to come from somewhere down the road. He walked quickly in the direction from which it came, and on the other side of a low hedge a sorry spectacle met his gaze.

Miss Frayle had fallen into a pond, half hidden by weed and grass. It seemed to be filled to a depth of about three feet, for she was up to well above her waist in muddy, stagnant water, and was floundering about in an attempt to negotiate the steep bank. So far poor Miss Frayle had failed.

Doctor Morelle looked down at her with a sardonic smile at the corners of his mouth.

'Whatever are you doing there, Miss Frayle? Do you suddenly imagine yourself to be a newt?'

'I — I fell in,' she informed him unnecessarily. 'I thought this might be a shortcut, and was looking back to see if you were coming — ' She forced the words through chattering teeth.

'How long do you propose to continue your ablutions?' he queried as she splashed about in a vain attempt to pull herself out.

'Instead of asking silly questions, couldn't you help me?' she said miserably, half crying with mortification.

Suddenly from behind them came the

sound of rapid footsteps, and a voice approaching called out:

'Someone in trouble there?'

A well-built, middle-aged man appeared out of the gloom. He stopped on seeing them. 'Oh, hello,' he said, and then coming forward again offered in a friendly voice: 'Can I help?'

'Good evening,' replied Doctor Morelle calmly. 'Merely my assistant investigating pond life.'

The newcomer seemed rather mystified by the Doctor's explanation. He gave him a sharp look, then glanced at the shivering Miss Frayle.

'Better give her a hand, hadn't we?' he suggested.

'I was about to do so.'

'Come on then, I'll help. Catch hold, young lady, and we'll have you out in a jiffy.' And he extended his hand. Miss Frayle thankfully grasped it.

'Heave ho!' the man exclaimed heartily, and in a second she was standing on the bank, gasping for breath.

'My word, you're wet all right!' he said, looking at her dripping clothes, muddy and weed-bedraggled.

'Ye — yes — the water's terribly cold,' she replied through chattering teeth.

'You'd better come along to my place at once,' the man went on briskly. 'Cottage just across the field — you can dry your clothes and knock back a warm drink.'

'You're very kind,' chattered Miss Frayle gratefully. She adjusted her spectacles which had fallen awry during her misadventure, and made a wan attempt to smile her gratitude at him through the mud and water-bespattered lenses.

'What d'you say, sir?' The stranger turned to Doctor Morelle, who had stood there silent, surveying Miss Frayle and her rescuer with a saturnine expression.

'Yes,' he murmured condescendingly. 'I feel somewhat chilly myself. A little stimulant would prove very acceptable.'

'Come along then, let's hurry — we'll be there in five minutes . . . ' As he moved off he added: 'By the way, my name's Archer — Gilbert Archer.' Doctor Morelle made the necessary introductions for himself and Miss Frayle. The man led the way and they followed, Miss Frayle flapping her arms to restore the circulation.

The cottage proved to be a substantial, half-timbered low building, with attractive lounge, in which the Doctor and the man who had introduced himself as Gilbert Archer sat before their drinks. Before them blazed a cheerful log fire. Presently, they were joined by Miss Frayle, clad in a huge dressing-gown, the property of her host, who insisted on lending it to her while her clothes dried over a clothes-horse in front of a great stove in the kitchen.

Archer was a man of obviously cultured tastes, and an agreeable hour was passed before Miss Frayle was attired once more in her own clothes. She and Doctor Morelle rose to go, and he turned to thank the man.

'Well, Mr. Archer . . . Rest assured Miss Frayle and I are greatly indebted to you for your hospitality.'

'Yes,' added Miss Frayle gratefully, and suppressing a sneeze, 'you have been most kind.'

'Not a bit,' he answered genially. 'Afraid you're in for a cold, Miss Frayle . . . I've been only too glad of your company. You see, I've been in Bleakcliff only a few weeks, and are people here sticky to know!'

'The natives appear to be somewhat unfriendly?' queried Doctor Morelle with an expressive lift of the eyebrows.

'Rotten, miserable lot of snobs, that's what they are!' burst out Archer viciously, knocking out the ash from an old pipe. He realised that he must have appeared rather vehement, and with an apologetic smile he subsided.

'Sorry, I didn't mean to let fly like that! But I am a little bitter about 'em. Downright unpleasant, they've been. Give you an example: Only this evening, just before I saw you, I met a fellow named Carpenter, who lives at the big house along the way. My nearest neighbour. We met point-blank in the lane — not another soul in sight. D'you think he'd wish me 'Good evening'? Not on your life! That's the sort of people they are. Because they live in a bigger house, or have been here forty years, or happen to be second cousin to a bishop — !' he broke off with a shrug. 'There — I'm at it again.'

'What a shame!' sympathised Miss Frayle in slightly muffled voice, 'I'm so sorry, Mr. Archer.'

Doctor Morelle, however, shook his head, his expression censorious:

'I feel your attitude indicates a somewhat scanty understanding of human behaviour,' he pronounced. He paused, then said through a puff of cigarette-smoke: 'Somewhat incomprehensible, Mr. Archer, in one who would seem to be a student of psychology.' He indicated the large book-cases round the walls, where there was row upon row of formidable volumes.

'Oh, you've noticed my little library?' said Archer. 'Yes, I've studied the subject deeply, and still read everything on it I can.'

Doctor Morelle crossed over to a bookshelf and thoughtfully scanned its contents.

'Um . . . Freud . . . Jung . . . Adler . . . and the other school, I see . . . Watson . . .

Pavlov . . . ' He turned to the other with a curious little smile. 'You have delved deeply into the subconscious!'

At this point Miss Frayle found it humanly impossible any longer to suppress a gigantic sneeze.

'Almost as deeply as Miss Frayle delved into the pond,' the Doctor added, with a sardonic glance in her direction.

'It's a fascinating subject,' Archer said with enthusiasm.

'The investigation of any mystery is fascinating,' Doctor Morelle said absently, moving away from the bookshelf and thoughtfully tapping the ash off his Le Sphinx. 'Especially when one sees its elucidation near.'

If Miss Frayle had not been too preoccupied with her cold, she might have detected an implication in his words. But they seemed to have fallen on empty air.

Soon afterwards, Doctor Morelle and Miss Frayle wished Gilbert Archer goodnight, and hurried on their way back to Arthur Hall's house. They arrived there without any further mishap. Their host would not hear of their returning to London that night; it was by now dark and the night uninviting for travelling. He had already prepared their rooms for them, he assured them, and Miss Frayle was thankful to retire with a hot water bottle and a glass of hot milk.

'I should like to use your telephone before I partake of some supper,' Doctor Morelle said to the other after Miss Frayle had gone upstairs.

Hall looked at him interrogatively, but the Doctor gave no explanation for his request.

'Yes . . . yes. Of course!' Hall suddenly realised he had not answered him. 'Can I help you find the number?'

'That will not be necessary,' the Doctor suavely assured him. 'I merely wish to telephone the Police Station.'

★ ★ ★

Doctor Morelle, Miss Frayle — little the worse for her experience of the previous evening — and Hall, were finishing breakfast the next morning, when they heard a sound in the drive outside. Miss Frayle recognised Sergeant Preedy, his face glowing with exertion and excitement, pedal energetically up to the front door. He had rung the bell and been admitted into the room almost before she had announced that it was he.

'We got him, Doctor — we got him!' He gasped for breath, mopping his brow. 'Caught him red-handed right outside Major Carpenter's front door. Just like you said!' He grinned in open admiration at the Doctor. 'Though how you found him out is a mystery! A quiet feller like that . . . Last person I'd suspect . . . ' He went burbling on excitedly.

A cryptic smile flickered for a moment across Doctor Morelle's saturnine features. 'It's rather too long a story, Sergeant Preedy,' he said quietly. 'And I have to go up in a moment to see my patient, Mrs. Hall. Then I must return to Town without delay.' And he went out of the room, leaving the Sergeant scratching his head in bewilderment and Miss Frayle goggling at Hall blankly.

Later, Sergeant Preedy had departed,

and Arthur Hall was saying to the Doctor with a puzzled air:

'And you really mean to say that this man Archer sent those poison-pen cards?'

'Undoubtedly.'

'But — but we hardly know the man.'

'That was a contributory cause of the trouble.' With that enigmatic utterance Doctor Morelle seemed to dismiss the matter from his mind, and went on to reassure the other that his wife's recovery was merely a matter of a week or two's rest. The shadow that had suddenly darkened her life was as suddenly swept away.

On the return journey, Miss Frayle was silent for some time. Presently, however, she turned to him, her face puzzled. 'I still can't see how you found out about Mr. Archer,' she said.

He bestowed a condescending smile on her. He said:

'It was merely a question of taking each piece of the jigsaw and fitting them together until one outstanding factor emerged. This was that the writer of the postcards was in each case unaware whether or not the recipients actually had a guilty secret. Otherwise the nature of the crime would obviously have been stated in order to achieve the maximum effect of fear in the intended victim. All the postcards, however, referred to 'your crime' and nothing more.' Keeping one hand on the steering wheel, he contrived dexterously to take out his cigarette case, extract a Le Sphinx and light it.

'The writer was obviously a person of some education,' he went on through a cloud of cigarette smoke, 'which narrowed the list of suspects. The motive was not of a mercenary nature, nor with intent to discredit the recipient with the outside world. Each card, you may recall, was delivered, not through the post, but privately. It would appear, therefore, the poison-pen writer was a person who, without knowing them very intimately, bore a grudge against a number of Bleakcliff's most prominent inhabitants, and out of revenge merely aimed at frightening them. That person, moreover, was a student of the human mind; someone who realised that almost without exception every one of us suffers from a latent sense of guilt — the universal guilt complex which lurks in the subconscious.'

'And of course Mr. Archer was a student of human nature,' she remembered. 'All those books he had on psychology and all that.'

'Precisely, my dear Miss Frayle.'

There followed a short silence. She seemed to be wrestling with some intricate problem. Then:

'Of course, you were right, Doctor Morelle — I know — '

'Thank you!'

'But — ' she went on determinedly, ' — but we don't all have these 'guilt complexes' you speak about — '

'No?' He gave her a sardonic look.

'No,' she said firmly. 'I mean — '

He interrupted her. 'That reminds me,' he said in an off-hand tone. 'Scotland Yard telephoned this morning before we left for London.' He went on, with a sinister emphasis: 'They asked for you —!'

'Scotland Yard?' she exclaimed.

'I decided I would not mention it to you at the time — '

She went pale. 'But why — ? What have I done — ?'

And then she realised his face was twisted with repressed saturnine amusement. 'My dear Miss Frayle!' he chuckled, 'how white you have gone! Can it be that even you have a guilty secret?'

Indignantly she said: 'No, no! Of course not — !'

'Nevertheless,' he mocked her, 'your subconscious guilt would seem to be working at full pressure! As indeed it does with everyone . . .'

Miss Frayle glared at him through her spectacles. Still chuckling delightedly at the manner in which he had succeeded in making an example of her to prove his argument, Doctor Morelle pressed his foot on the accelerator and the car sped onwards towards London.

# 7

## The Case of the Missing Treasury Official

A vacation in the accepted sense was rarely in the scheme of things so far as Doctor Morelle was concerned. True, for an odd week or two during the year he was not to be found at the house in Harley Street, but those weeks were never spent in complete isolation from all things scientific. Rather did he prefer to utilise the time away from London on some research. Research, for example, in a branch of science which he had little opportunity of pursuing in the midst of his many activities and investigations which kept him busy most of the time.

When he intimated to Miss Frayle they were to devote the middle fortnight in July to a journey to the small Aegean island of K — , she asked in her shy, tentative manner what inquiry he proposed to make there. In vain, she sought to recall any mention of the island in correspondence — or even a telephone call. She could think of none, and when he urbanely assured her that he had decided to visit K — because he liked it at that time of year, her spectacles almost slipped off her nose in a sudden joyful anticipation of a real holiday at last.

But the Doctor had not informed her why he liked K — in July. It had nothing to do with the uninterrupted sunshine, or the soft warm breezes, or even the incomparable blueness of the ocean around its sandy beaches.

They had scarcely established themselves at the main hotel on the island before the truth was out. Doctor Morelle introduced her to a bulky specimen case that he had unpacked immediately. He proceeded to inform her they would be spending the greater part of their time in search of certain fauna that were to be found on the rocks in the hot July sun instead of taking refuge in the crevices and fissures that concealed them for the greater part of the year.

Assuming that K — would prove to be a miniature Lido, Miss Frayle had brought high-heeled shoes and two new dresses that she felt were most appropriate. On hearing the Doctor's plans for their stay she swallowed her chagrin and with commendable commonsense hurried out and purchased a serviceable ready-made skirt and short-sleeved shirt, together with a pair of sandals. In the days to come she was to congratulate herself time and again upon her foresight in making this rapid decision.

Clad in a pair of flannels, an old shirt and a large Panama hat, Doctor Morelle proved absolutely tireless. Hour after hour he scrambled over jagged rocks, occasionally pausing to peer through a magnifying glass that he carried in his hip pocket. He lectured Miss Frayle unceasingly upon the habits of crustacean life that she had never known to exist. She remained unconvinced that she was any the happier for the knowledge imparted to her by the energetic Doctor. For the first day or two, she simulated some interest in the various specimens, even managed to ask what she thought were several intelligent questions. At the end of that time, however, she was more concerned with her freckles and sunburn to worry very much about the various data relative to such insignificant creatures with their long Latin names and to her, uninteresting histories.

Doctor Morelle seemed as usual, either quite unaware of or indifferent to her boredom. He continued his scientific harangues as if he were conducting a party of students. Every day, the routine was the same, and they arrived back at the hotel just in time to take a bath and change for dinner, after which Doctor Morelle would disappear to pore over the specimens he had captured that day, and make copious notes concerning them. Left behind in the hotel lounge, Miss Frayle would drowsily listen to the small orchestra until she could repel sleep no longer. She would sleep to dream often of myriads of nightmarish versions of the odd creatures which had fascinated Doctor Morelle during the day's scramble over the beach and rocks.

One evening at dinner, Miss Frayle noticed a strikingly attractive woman eyeing the Doctor speculatively. She was dark and exotic-looking, and sat at a conspicuous table by one of the windows. She was alone. Miss Frayle sighed, not without a trace of envy as she observed her well-moulded high cheekbones, long lashes and perfectly proportioned nose. She noticed the woman looked across at the door every time anyone entered, as if she expected a companion to join her. No one had done so, however, when Miss Frayle and the Doctor adjourned to the lounge for their coffee.

The little orchestra was playing a soft melodious folk air with a romantic lilt which Miss Frayle hummed to herself as she sipped her coffee. The Doctor eyed her over his Le Sphinx with an expression of annoyance. He was anxious to discuss certain discoveries he had made that day, though he was, of course, perfectly aware Miss Frayle was quite indifferent to these researches. He was about to interpose a cutting remark which would dissolve her not unmelodious accompaniment to the orchestra when a waiter appeared, hesitated a moment, then came across to them with a note. He stood in anticipation as Doctor Morelle tore open the pale mauve envelope, asking as he did so:

'Who gave you this?'

'That lady over there, Doctor Morelle,' the waiter indicated with a movement of his head the woman whom Miss Frayle had noticed earlier. She was now having coffee in a corner. She was still alone. The Doctor threw a narrowed glance in her direction.

'H'm,' he murmured, unfolding the single sheet of notepaper, 'I am not under the impression I have made her acquaintance.'

'Well, she's certainly been trying to make yours!' put in Miss Frayle, who had been watching the proceedings with some interest. 'I've noticed the looks she's been giving you.'

He turned and swept her with a sardonic look.

'I am gratified to learn of the interest you have taken upon my behalf,' he said.

Miss Frayle, too intrigued with the situation, remained for once unabashed.

'What's in her note?' she asked. 'Perhaps she wants to show you the ruins by moonlight!'

'I have no interest in expeditions of an archaeological nature,' he assured her seriously. He assumed an air of indifference and seemed about to return the note to the waiter without reading it.

Miss Frayle sighed.

'Do read it!' she urged.

'Curiously enough, ruins have never appealed to my intellect,' mused the Doctor, as if considering this phenomenon for the first time. 'There is no doubt a psychological reason — but that would of course defy the comprehension of a minor intelligence such as yours, my dear Miss Frayle.'

His voice trailed into a murmur. The waiter, abandoning all hope of a reply to the message, withdrew. Very deliberately, Doctor Morelle laid the note on the table and tapped the ash off his cigarette. After a moment's pause he picked up the note again. Miss Frayle noticed his eyes narrow and a wary expression flicker over his saturnine features.

''Dear Doctor Morelle',' he read quietly, with a slight frown. ''Forgive this presumption, but I am in great distress, and know you can help me. If you will, follow me out into the hotel courtyard. I will explain everything. Believe me, Lola Varetta'.'

'The notepaper's got rather a nice faint perfume,' remarked Miss Frayle.

'Thank you, but my own olfactory organ is not completely insensitive and is capable of detecting the aroma to which you refer!'

'What are you going to do?' she said, ignoring his familiarly pompous sarcasm.

He replaced the note in its envelope and puffed thoughtfully at his cigarette. 'It is, of course, always difficult to ignore an SOS, however obscure its origin,' he murmured.

'And besides she is very lovely . . . '

'My dear Miss Frayle, feminine pulchritude makes an impression upon me so infinitesimal it might well be described as negligible.'

'All the same,' she persisted, 'you're going to follow her!'

He smiled at her thinly: 'And I presume that if I do you will be able to pride yourself upon an intimate knowledge of human reactions?'

He drank the rest of his coffee slowly. Suddenly Miss Frayle said in a whisper: 'Look! She's going out now!'

He said slowly in a studiously absent tone: 'I think, however, you might post-pone any observations upon the problems of human conduct until a more propitious moment.' And he rose to his feet. Miss Frayle set down her cup quickly.

'Doctor Morelle — are you going?'

'An acute observer like yourself should have no need to ask such a question!' he retorted.

'She's gone in the direction of the courtyard!'

'You grow more observant each year!'

'I'd better come with you,' she said determinedly, standing beside him.

'Do indeed. Let us find her together in the — er — trysting place she has chosen.'

Glancing at her worried face and eyes apprehensive behind her spectacles, he chuckled sardonically, and led the way in the direction in which the woman had disappeared.

The courtyard was small, and black shadows lay on one side cast by the brilliant moonlight. The air was sweet and heavy with the scent of flowers.

'Is that you, Doctor Morelle?' came a soft, liquid voice from out of the shadows. It possessed the merest trace of a foreign accent. Miss Frayle thought it held a somewhat caressing note that filled her with a vague sense of irritation.

'Good evening,' murmured the Doctor.

'Oh, how can I thank you!' cried Lola Varetta, impulsively, coming forward into the moonlight, her hands outstretched.

'This is my assistant, Miss Frayle,' he introduced.

Miss Frayle said politely: 'How do you do?'

The woman halted. 'Good evening,' she responded with much less enthusiasm, which did not pass unnoticed by Miss Frayle. A tiny smile appeared at the corners of her mouth and hovered there.

'It would appear that you are in need of help, Miss Varetta?' said the Doctor.

In her emotion the other's hand went to her slender white throat. 'It is terrible — terrible! I am almost out of my senses.'

Doctor Morelle surveyed her for a moment. He murmured:

'Tell me quietly and calmly.'

Lola Varetta clutched his arm dramatically.

'Ah, Doctor! — how wonderful, how soothing your personality. The instant I saw you tonight, I realised your strength of character and your noble mind. I knew if only I could gain your help . . . And then when the waiter told me you were the great London doctor, the Great Doctor Morelle . . . '

Miss Frayle gave a little cough. Surely he can see she's just an adventuress telling the old, old story! she said to herself. But the Doctor gave no sign that he was in any way embarrassed by this fulsome flattery. On the contrary, a gratified expression seemed to flicker over his saturnine features. Or perhaps it was just a trick of the moonlight.

'You were telling me that you were in some distress,' he reminded her.

'Ah yes! It is my brother — he is lost — or — or dead!'

'Lost? But surely on a small island of this nature that would be somewhat difficult?'

'You do not understand. My brother should have returned from the Bullion Vaults by now. He was to have met me here at the hotel. I have a premonition — '

'Bullion Vaults?' He cut into the rapidly rising note of hysteria in her voice.

'Yes.' She spoke more slowly, calmed by his tone. 'He should have returned this evening from the Bullion Vaults at the usual time. They are at the Treasury, my brother is a Treasury official. I telephoned there several times, but no answer.'

'When did you last telephone?'

'About an hour ago.'

'But surely a night watchman is on duty?'

'Still there is no answer. That is why I feel certain something is wrong.'

'You say you telephoned your brother several times?'

'Yes . . . First about four-thirty and an official told me he was not in. I thought perhaps he had gone out to tea at one of the ministries, so I did not telephone again until after six o'clock. He had not returned then. The official I had spoken to before was just leaving. He said my brother had told him when he went out that he would return a little later. He could not understand what had delayed my brother. Again I telephoned, as I have told you, about an hour ago. Oh, what should I do, Doctor Morelle? Please, please help me!'

'Why not get the police?' It was Miss Frayle who, somewhat to her surprise, found herself making the suggestion. She promptly stammered and then fell silent, fiddling with her spectacles in embarrassment at having spoken at all. Lola Varetta seemed momentarily to be taken aback by the question.

'Perhaps I had better explain,' she murmured, after some hesitation.

'That,' replied Doctor Morelle crisply,

211

'would be an excellent idea!'

'You will understand, Doctor . . . ' she hesitated again, then went on. 'My brother is a little unpopular with the police authorities. There was a big forgery case recently in which he was called to give evidence — he is something of an expert in such matters. As it happened, his evidence was not favourable to the police as they had anticipated. Their prisoner was not convicted.' She spread her hands expressively — 'They have not forgotten! So I do not wish to involve my brother in an enquiry that may turn out to be of no importance. That is why I ask you to investigate. The police are — ' she forced a wan smile — 'how you say, not very clever. They would be clumsy and stupid. But you, you are discreet and so clever.'

She gave him the full benefit of her smile, and her eyes shone with admiration.

Miss Frayle gave a little cough that might have been a discreet comment, or merely caused by a tickling in her throat. Doctor Morelle glanced at her sharply.

'Where are the Bullion Vaults?' he asked Lola Varetta.

'On the other side of the town,' she replied quickly. 'I have my car ready. We could drive there at once.' She sensed the possibility that her appeal for help had not fallen on stony ground. 'Oh, Doctor!' she exclaimed. 'You are so wonderful — !'

'Very well, let us proceed,' he cut in hurriedly. 'I feel sure, of course, your brother has merely been detained.' He turned to Miss Frayle: 'No doubt you would appreciate a drive in this — ah — romantic moonlight in any case. Would you not?'

'I think I might enjoy it very much,' she replied in a tone that was somewhat non-committal. He eyed her with a sardonic smile.

'You would like your assistant to accompany us?' the woman asked with a show of surprise. 'In case there may be some danger?' she insinuated.

'I think there may be some danger if I don't,' answered Miss Frayle quickly and with surprising finality. She had already made up her mind. The entire story was a concoction from start to finish!

Lola Varetta's car proved to be a large, expensive-looking one, scarlet in colour. It purred through the narrow moonlit streets.

Doctor Morelle sat, at her inescapable invitation, beside the glamorous creature, who handled the wheel skilfully. Miss Frayle was in the back, straining her ears to catch every word of their conversation. It appeared, however, to consist of little more than a cross-examination by the Doctor on the habits and routine of the missing brother. A few minutes brought them to the Bullion Vaults.

It was an old building of ornate type of architecture. It loomed massive and darkly forbidding in the shadows of the narrow street in which it was situated. Lola Varetta stopped the car outside the front entrance, and almost before the sound of the engine had died away she had hurried up the broad steps and tried the heavy studded door. It was locked.

'You see! It is locked!' she cried.

'Hardly surprising in the case of a

Bullion Vaults,' remarked Doctor Morelle dryly. He stepped back and surveyed the front of the building for any sign of life. All the windows were dark.

'I presume there is some sort of side entrance?' he asked, 'A smaller door reserved for employees?'

'I — I do not know — '

'Let us investigate.'

Followed by the woman and Miss Frayle, he led the way round one side of the building and down an even narrower street. There were indeed two smaller doors, but the first they tried was locked. The second, however, stood half-open. A breath of chill air seemed to meet them. The Doctor paused for a moment and eyed the entrance thoughtfully. He lit a Le Sphinx before observing: 'Presumably we may enter!' Taking a small torch from his pocket he led the way into a bare looking small and chilly vestibule

Miss Frayle shivered. 'It seems very quiet in there — and dark,' she whispered. She and the woman stood looking round uncertainly. There were three doors leading from the little hallway, all of them closed. There was a small reception cubicle in a corner near the door they had just entered. Doctor Morelle flashed his torch inside it. It was empty.

'Something is wrong!' gasped Lola Varetta. She appeared obviously very scared. 'That door should have been locked.' She pointed to the door of the street. 'Something has happened to my brother!' Even Miss Frayle thought her distress was genuine. She herself was not feeling particularly happy. There seemed to be an atmosphere of chill foreboding about their surroundings. She wished she was back in the hotel.

'Come now, calm yourself,' murmured Doctor Morelle. 'Perhaps if you would both remain here while I investigate a little further — '

He was moving in the direction of the right-hand door when it opened suddenly and a wide beam of light from a large torch swept over them. When the light had moved from his eyes, the Doctor could discern two men had appeared. They were wearing police uniforms. One of them carried an old-fashioned portmanteau. The leading man addressed them sharply in the island tongue. When Doctor Morelle answered imperiously in English that he did not speak that language, the second man spoke:

'What are you doing here, and who are you?' he said in harsh accents. It was he who carried the torch and he waved it aggressively.

Lola answered coolly, and in English for the benefit of her companions: 'I am calling for my brother — Captain Varetta of the Treasury Staff.'

The man surveyed her. 'Captain Varetta would not be here at this hour,' he said with a meaning smile. 'You say he is your brother, eh? And tell me, please, how are we to know that? You have opened that door — you and these people with you may be thieves — '

'A party of thieves intent upon robbing your vaults would hardly consist of one man and two very harmless women!' murmured Doctor Morelle. 'And please refrain from shining that torch in my face. I find it extremely trying to the eyes.'

The man ceased shining the torch haphazardly. He looked at his companion questioningly, as if awaiting a decision. The other came forward a pace.

'I am afraid,' he said in halting English, which they found difficult to follow. 'You stay here until I make further inquiries. Please do not leave here. Please!' He turned to the other man and spoke sharply. 'You stay outside the door — come!'

The two men in uniform went out into the street, closing the door after them.

'Are we imprisoned?' asked Miss Frayle apprehensively, the moment they had gone. The Doctor silenced her with a look. Cautiously he approached the window and appeared to be listening intently. Then he suddenly opened the outer door through which the men had made their purposeful exit. He came back, threw his cigarette to the floor and crushed it with his heel.

'As I had apprehended. Both have disappeared!'

'Both?' echoed Lola Varetta.

'Disappeared!' gulped Miss Frayle,

goggling at him through her spectacles.

'Do you mean they were not — real policemen?' cried the other.

'I entertain that very strong suspicion. Had they been, why did they not, for instance, demand from us some means of identification?' He glanced at Lola Varetta.

'But their uniforms — ?' stammered Miss Frayle.

'My dear Miss Frayle, you really must refrain from such ingenuous acceptance of the obvious. Does it not occur to even your simple imagination that it might be possible for determined persons anxious to impersonate minions of the law to procure uniforms very similar to, if not actually, those of the police?'

'But how could they — ?' Lola Varetta was beginning to ask further questions when he once again waved a hand for silence. 'Listen!'

From the front of the building came the unmistakable sound of a powerful motor engine.

'My car!' exclaimed Lola. 'How dare they . . .'

Doctor Morelle made a little gesture of resignation.

'I fear it is too late now to take action,' he murmured. 'Apart, of course, from telephoning the police. The real police,' he added with a faint smile. 'Perhaps you would be good enough to do so from the nearest callbox. I seem to remember observing one just outside this building. Do not concern yourself unduly. Your vehicle will be recovered.' As she turned to do so, he called after her: 'For the time being, it will be sufficient to report the theft of your car.'

She nodded. 'Yes, yes, I quite understand, Doctor Morelle. Of course . . . ' She hurried out.

The Doctor turned to Miss Frayle. 'The theft of her car seems to have taken her mind off the whereabouts of her brother,' he remarked. 'Which may be as well.'

'What — what do you think has happened to him?'

'That, my dear Miss Frayle, is a matter for my immediate investigation.' He moved to the door through which the two men posing as police officials had made their appearance. 'Would you care to remain here and await Miss Varetta's return? Or accompany me?'

Miss Frayle gulped.

'I think I'll come with you, Doctor Morelle.'

'There may be a body or two,' Doctor Morelle warned her with a thin smile.

'I — I'd rather be with you,' she admittedly nervously.

He regarded her with raised eyebrows and, in a tone of over-elaborate surprise, said: 'Indeed?'

Miss Frayle said, as if to explain her admission: 'I — I don't think she likes me . . . '

'I see!' And with a sardonic glance at her he went swiftly through the door. She followed him, keeping as close behind him as possible, wondering what it was this time, what it was she could have said which, it appeared, had offended him.

No sooner had he proceeded a few steps along the passage than the Doctor saw a reflected light in the distance. He hastened in its direction, to reach a short flight of steps. These led to a cellar where the light was burning. It was similar in appearance to any underground room in a bank or safe deposit vaults, with its long rows of files. There was also an ancient copying press, a badly scarred desk and an odd chair or two.

On the opposite side of the room, Doctor Morelle saw what he sought — a formidable iron door, resplendent with the coat of arms favoured by the makers of the strong room.

'This is, I feel, the Bullion Chamber,' he informed Miss Frayle, as he strode over to examine the door.

'If it is, I don't see how we can possibly break into it!' said Miss Frayle, whose confidence had returned somewhat, for that seemed to be his intention.

'No?' he replied. 'Nevertheless might we not attempt a not unconventional method of gaining admittance!' He swung his weight on the handle, and the massive door slowly opened outwards to Miss Frayle's astonishment.

'It — it couldn't have been locked!' she gasped, pushing her spectacles, which, in her excitement had slipped awry, back into place. The Doctor for once made no attempt to administer one of his invariably crushing replies. He was intent upon the figure of a man leaning against the bars of the inner gate. Obviously it was the night watchman. The man was conscious though he appeared somewhat overcome by the heavy atmosphere in the strong room, which had only one small ventilator. However, the outside air that now found its way into the Bullion Chamber seemed to revive him. By the aid of the light from the outer cellar Doctor Morelle could discern an inert form in a corner. A gasp from behind him signified Miss Frayle had seen it too.

'Who — who is that?' she breathed.

The night watchman, groaning and with a dazed expression, answered her in broken English.

'It is — Captain Varetta.' He went on speaking with difficulty. 'I am the night watchman. I came on duty at six o'clock this evening. All was quiet. Then Captain Varetta returned for some papers. That would be about seven o'clock. I was

223

saying goodnight to him — just outside in the passage there — when two men in policemen's uniforms suddenly appeared and attacked us. They threw us in here and imprisoned us behind these bars.'

Doctor Morelle nodded.

'We have, in fact, just seen two men such as you describe. We shall have to find some way of extricating you,' he added, eyeing the heavy lock from which the key had been removed. 'I fear I am powerless to unlock this.'

'Ah, the scoundrels took the key! Doubtless they have robbed the other bullion rooms as well,' the man said with a dejected expression.

'I see you consoled yourself and helped to pass the time by smoking,' observed Doctor Morelle, glancing through the bars and noting the stubs littered around the floor.

'I was so upset — it helped to quiet my nerves. I smoked all I had — there were only three.'

'Better take one of mine till we can find somebody to let you out.' The Doctor handed him his case through the bars, and offered the flame from his lighter. The man accepted the cigarette gratefully.

'Thank you — thank you — ' he murmured, inhaling deeply. 'When I recovered consciousness — it would be about half-an-hour ago, I found myself in here with — with Captain Varetta.' He looked at the inanimate figure in the corner. 'He was already dead,' he said soberly.

'So I had already perceived,' said Doctor Morelle. 'He appears to have suffered a fatal blow on the head.' He paused for a moment to gaze at the body. Then he asked: 'What are your instructions in an emergency such as this?'

'Telephone the police. The number is N004801.'

'N004801,' echoed Miss Frayle automatically.

'Is there a telephone near at hand?'

'There is a switchboard in the second room along this corridor.'

Doctor Morelle turned to Miss Frayle: 'Perhaps you will telephone the police. I do not have to instruct you to advise them to come immediately.' But Miss

Frayle had hurried off almost before he had finished speaking. She was not unhappy to quit the scene of the violent and murderous attack that had resulted in Captain Varetta's death, and the prospect of doing something useful calmed her shaky nerves.

The police arrived ten minutes later to find Doctor Morelle and Miss Frayle reviving Lola Varetta. She had collapsed at the sight of her brother. She had rushed into the Bullion Vault before Miss Frayle could intercept her to break the news more gently. When the officer in charge of the several policemen who had arrived had liberated the night watchman, Doctor Morelle said to the former:

'I want you to examine the contents of Captain Varetta's pockets.' He indicated the dead man, and he and the officer together carefully examined his clothing. Their search revealed a wallet, a gold watch, a silver pencil and fountain pen, a handkerchief, keys, some small silver and two or three personal letters.

'Nothing much there,' commented the officer.

Doctor Morelle nodded thoughtfully. He turned to the night watchman and suddenly snapped:

'Be good enough to turn out your pockets!'

The man looked surprised, but with a look at the police officer he slowly obeyed. There were a few coins, a handkerchief, a penknife, notebook and an envelope containing identity papers.

'That is all?' queried Doctor Morelle.

The man nodded. 'But yes,' he said with an attempt at a smile. 'What else should there be?'

Looking a trifle puzzled, the officer turned deferentially to the Doctor. 'I do not understand what you expect to find,' he said.

'No? Then perhaps you will be good enough to examine the floor of this strong room.'

Very mystified, the others obeyed.

'What do you find there?' queried Doctor Morelle.

'Only three cigarette ends,' was the baffled reply.

'That is all the evidence necessary,'

murmured the Doctor, 'to implicate this man — ' he indicated the night watchman, whose jaw sagged — 'in the murder of Captain Varetta and the theft of the bullion which was removed by his confederates tonight.'

Doctor Morelle calmly proceeded to light a Le Sphinx while the others stared at him in amazement. The night watchman was the first to recover from his surprise, but as he made a move to escape, Miss Frayle gave a warning cry and the man was forcibly restrained by three policemen, and a pair of handcuffs clamped on him.

The Doctor puffed luxuriously at his cigarette. 'And now,' he said, 'I must attend to the deceased's sister.'

★　★　★

Under the influence of a prescription given to her by Doctor Morelle, Lola Varetta had at last sunk into an exhausted sleep. With an expression of satisfaction, the Doctor turned to Miss Frayle:

'Miss Varetta will sleep now. Tomorrow

I will visit her again — ' They were in her own bedroom of her villa overlooking the shore. 'I fear that unless she takes my advice, which I shall of course persuade her to do, she may suffer a bad breakdown in health.'

'Poor woman. What a terrible thing to have happened!' He nodded. 'I shall have to call at police headquarters for a few minutes in the morning first. Then, after I have visited Miss Varetta here I shall be free to continue my researches into the life and death of those crustacean creatures which I pointed out to you this morning, Miss Frayle. You will recall the species in particular which I suggested bore a certain resemblance to human beings, in that some types appeared almost to be guided by good intentions and others by evil intentions, and all met a similar fate that seemed designed for them . . . ?'

When they arrived back at their hotel, a message awaited Doctor Morelle asking him to telephone a number. He returned five minutes later.

'As I expected, the man has confessed,'

he said to Miss Frayle. 'His two confederates have been overtaken by a police launch heading for the mainland.'

She was very tired by the night's events, but not too wearied to ask:

'But I still don't see how you discovered the night watchman was mixed up in the crime.'

'Merely a matter of logical application to all the essential facts in the case. The man claimed to have regained consciousness some thirty minutes prior to my opening the door of the Bullion Chamber. During that time he smoked three cigarettes — you may recall there were three remains of them on the floor. But neither I nor the police officers found any spent matches. On searching the deceased and the night watchman, furthermore, neither proved to possess either matches or lighter.' He paused, then said softly: 'How then did the night watchman ignite his first cigarette?'

Miss Frayle gasped.

'You mean he must have got a light from one of the two men — before he was locked in the strong room?'

'Precisely. Which fact pointed to his story being false — and his implication in the crime. As he has confessed, he was in actuality party with the other two men to an elaborately planned robbery. Out of this Captain Varetta's murder — unpremeditated no doubt — was a result.'

Miss Frayle shuddered:

'How terrible!'

The Doctor went on smoothly: 'As I shall now be able to dispense with my visit to police headquarters, I feel it would be beneficial if I made an early start for that part of the shore I was investigating. No doubt you will wish to accompany me, Miss Frayle?'

Her heart sank at the prospect.

'Immediately after breakfast, do you not agree?' his voice went on remorselessly in her ear. 'An early breakfast . . . '

She had been looking forward to enjoying a late breakfast in bed. She stammered, started to ask him if he might not prefer to start off alone. The words stuck in her throat.

'You wish to say something?'

'I — I — that is — ' She gave up. 'Oh,

all right, Doctor Morelle,' she said.

'Goodnight, Miss Frayle.'

'Goodnight, Doctor . . . ' And Miss Frayle sighed heavily and stumbled wearily upstairs to bed.

## THE END

DR. MORELLE MEETS MURDER
A CASE FOR DR. MORELLE
DR. MORELLE'S CASEBOOK
DR. MORELLE INVESTIGATES
DR. MORELLE INTERVENES
SEND FOR DR. MORELLE
DR. MORELLE ELUCIDATES